T0036592

nine

by Blag Dahlia

RARE BIRD
LOS ANGELES, CALIF.

THIS IS A GENUINE RARE BIRD BOOK

Rare Bird Books
6044 North Figueroa Street
Los Angeles, CA 90042
rarebirdbooks.com

REVISED TRADE PAPERBACK ORIGINAL EDITION

PREVIOUSLY PUBLISHED IN 2006 BY GREEDY

Rare Bird Books Subsidiary Rights Department
6044 North Figueroa Street
Los Angeles, CA 90042

Cover Art by Zoe Lacchei

Design by Dana Collins

Set in Baskerville
Printed in the United States

10 9 8 7 6 5 4 3 2 1

Publisher's Cataloging-in-Publication Data available upon request.

"Compassion is wasted on those who need it."
—R. P. Cafaro III

1

These Kids Today

LINDA MURPHY WIPED HER hands on the rough pink of her apron and turned toward the sound of the ringing doorbell. When Marshall had called to say that he was entertaining clients downtown, and asked if she would like to spend the night in the city, she'd called the sitter straight away. Now Nina was here, right on time.

Not long ago the twins crying and carrying on would make Linda feel so guilty that she could barely leave the house at all. The disappointment in their eyes was more than she could stand just for a night out. But then she had found Nina West and things had begun to turn around.

In this age of flakes and foolishness Nina was rock solid, someone you could rely on even on short notice, even on a school night. Marshall trusted her and the kids loved her. She kept the house clean, never had boys over or chatted with friends on the phone. Really, she was almost too good to be true. Linda stole a look at herself in the mirror as she hurried down the hallway.

Not bad for thirty-six, she thought.

Delivering twins hadn't been easy, but it was nothing compared to those last twelve pounds. She'd given up meat and then dairy, taken up tennis, racquetball, and in a burst of frustration, Brazilian jiu-jitsu. Finally, she'd just given up eating anything before six or after eight and woe to anyone that showed up during feeding hours.

Hearing the bell, her son Jamie came tearing down the hall dripping bathwater, his little feet slapping against the parquet floor. Right behind him was Jodi, his little sister by two minutes and fourteen seconds, yelping ecstatically.

"Nina's here, Nina's here!" they squealed, almost knocking their mother off her feet in a mad dash for the door.

"Slow down guys, you'll get Nina all wet!"

At age fifteen Nina West stood five foot five inches tall, six feet in the heels that she hadn't worn yet. Her face was delicate, melancholy, with long dark hair and a Mona Lisa pout covering six thousand dollars worth of orthodontia that prevented her from smiling except maybe at gunpoint. It had been five years since Nina had given up dolls and ponies, two years since she'd worn a pair of blue jeans.

"Now, I've made them their dinner and you've got everything you'll need for breakfast tomorrow. Don't forget to feed Buster in the morning, two cups of the dry, half a can of the wet stuff, and please don't spoil them too much with sweets..."

Nina listened attentively, saying nothing and Linda Murphy kept talking as the door shut, her footsteps clattering down the asphalt driveway and into the street. Nina headed for the living room, the twins trailing under her feet and jabbering at the top of their voices.

"I want candy," said Jodi, her chubby little legs wobbling slightly in a pair of Little Mermaid pajamas.

"Me too, ice cream and candy!"

The babysitter felt her attention wander as she experienced the not unpleasant sensation of a mild epileptic seizure. For a full minute she stared at the wall and heard nothing but the empty vacuum of space roaring in her ears.

These miniature siestas from reality were one of the perks of being Nina, like doing whatever you wanted and not caring about the consequences, and as quickly as it had come the spell was gone. Nina considered again for a moment if there was anything that she really wanted.

"What we want's not what we get," she finally said.

Nina looked at the twins to see her words escape out their freshly washed ears and into that realm where things said that weren't understood float aimlessly forever. But, she could see them thinking, could see their tiny minds mulling over her last utterance like multiplication tables or the Pledge of Allegiance gone horribly wrong.

"You're weird," said Jamie and he laughed. "I want ice cream.

"Me too," said Jodi.

The babysitter basked for a moment in the glow of adoration from her young charges. As an old wooden clock chimed eight the television murmured an advertisement for something that she didn't want at all. Then, Nina West sprawled out on the living room sofa and pulled a pint of Häagen-Dazs Butter Pecan ice cream out of a coated paper freezer bag in her black vinyl purse.

She hiked her skirt up and placed a dollop of the cool white concoction on her freshly minted cleft, where it melted just like you or I would if we only had the chance.

"Come and get it," she said, her braces glinting in the blue light from the TV set.

2

Something
Like Sympathy

HIGHLAND OAKS WAS THE kind of town that people worked their entire lives to afford, only to realize how truly hateful it was once their children had escaped and they themselves retired to somewhere, anywhere that was warm. Neighbors were to be envied, feared or despised as circumstances dictated. Zoning laws required that every carefully planned tree exuded just enough oxygen to sustain the drama that played itself out behind every carefully planned home. Despite the best intentions of the town's founders though, there was always a little dirt behind the daydream.

Nina could not understand why she, a babysitter herself, needed someone to look after her while her parents vacationed. It was beyond insulting; it was a travesty. They had insisted that a week was too long for her to fend for herself, and her old sitter Larry had been kind enough to volunteer his services.

Nina liked to keep contact with other humans to an absolute minimum, and that went double for Lawrence David Fischer. Larry was the type of person who gave tediousness a bad name. Conversations with him tended to fall of their own weight in mid-sentence. He was painfully shy, a repository of earaches, acne, asthma, and every other malady that the under-twenty set was prone to.

With her mouth set in a militant scowl Nina grunted goodbye to her parents and acknowledged the unbearable presence of Larry. She looked to the wall where framed pictures from her childhood hung and willed them into oblivion.

Larry apologized, coughed, blew his nose, banged his elbow on the sofa and headed for the bathroom. Several seconds later a great clattering crash that sounded like a sound effect from an old radio show brought Nina to the scene.

"I'm sorry…I guess I didn't see the toilet there," said Larry.

Nina reconsidered her prohibition on laughing. After all it was at someone else's expense. Also, the sight of Larry, his head doused in water from the commode and a plunger tangled in between his scabby legs was enough to bring Mt. Rushmore down in a fit of hearty, boulder shaking guffaws.

"Larry, you're hopeless."

In that instant she saw her sitter for who he was, an idiot, and she knew that she would sleep with him and that he would enjoy it more than any single event in his whole wretched existence. She felt a power more staggering than any she had ever known, better even than the adjustable nozzle on the faucet of her bathtub.

She pulled Larry to his feet and kissed him until he drooled. Undaunted, she pulled him out into the hallway and took his shirt off. His hands tried vainly to cover his flabby chest, whose total lack of musculature gave him what could best be described as small, pubescent breasts. Nina now knew how he had acquired the nickname Eggnog and why, for Larry, gym class was much like a medieval torture.

For Nina these man-melons were a revelation. She ran her fingers over them and nibbled with a growing fascination.

Deflowering a hopeless nerd was accomplishment enough, but getting a pair of tits into the bargain? It was more than she had dared hope for. Larry's breathing had quieted to an asthmatic wheeze as he succumbed to Nina's desires with only the occasional whimper to signal his continued participation in the event.

Despite the Good Book's distaste for it, Larry had attempted self-gratification several times in the last few years, but had always stopped short when he found that the more excited he became the harder his nose ran. Nina instinctively straddled him, allowing his facial fluids to drip freely onto the carpet. His presence of mind had returned enough to realize for the first time that he was engaged in something that might charitably be called sex. When that fact began to sink in, he became paralyzed with fear.

The surprisingly robust erection that he had been sporting began to falter, and with it his hopes that he would lose his virginity. A lifetime of shyness and ineptitude began to flood his penis with a deep sense of foreboding. Nina knew that she had to work fast or risk destroying what remained of both Larry's self-esteem and his flimsy joystick. She began to suck at him and although his fear was still palpable, basic biology began to win out as he felt his withered mojo return.

"This is nice," thought Larry.

Nina regretted having started the whole process, but once engaged her sense of humor wouldn't allow her to stop. To pass the time she fantasized about Larry as a modern-day Christ nailed helplessly to a tree as she, a Roman noblewoman, sucked at his undeserving genitals. Just by orgasming he consigned himself to the fires of Hell for all Eternity. It didn't take him very long.

When the act was through Larry lay there prone in the hallway for almost an hour. His mind wandered over a life that could best be described as pathetic; the specters of team sports, school dances, spelling bees, field trips and interminable lunchtimes bringing back a flood of unpleasant memories. Now though, he was redeemed. He rose to his feet, walked to the kitchen and looked his paramour squarely in the eye as she ate from a bowl of popcorn liberally doused in butter and salt. With more conviction than he had ever mustered he said:

"Nina, I love you."

Nina looked at Larry and laughed out loud.

3

What You Wish For

FOR NINA WEST, SCHOOL was something to punctuate the time between waking and sleep, an excuse to put on a new outfit. She liked some subjects better than others, but she detested most of her instructors, and all of her classmates, with an enviable consistency. Mr. Bollinger was now Nina's favorite teacher because he had just put his tongue in her ear and whispered urgently:

"I need you so bad!"

When the bell had tolled the end of school for the day, educator and aspiring novelist Cyrus Bollinger had asked Nina to stay after class. After confessing an all-consuming passion for his moodiest pupil, he had felt like a modern Nabokov. For her part, Nina just needed something to do until three o'clock when her favorite soap opera started. The show was called Doctor's Hospice and it featured physicians who had sex with each other when their patients died or went into a coma. All kinds of other things happened too, but Nina didn't care what those other things were.

"Nina, I'm on fire for you. Just the way you hold your books or toss your hair, it thrills me each time you walk into the room. You must think I'm an old fool, but you're my Beatrice, my Desdemona…it's madness, but I must have you come what may!"

Nina not only thought that he was an old fool, she knew it. She also knew that it was pretty lame of him to say some other girls' names while he groped at her, but he did have a sort of bookish eccentricity that fairly screamed victim. Never one to be self-conscious, Nina liked a man who appeared overwhelmed by reality and Bollinger fit the bill, from his Mr. Rodgers sweater to his brown loafers to the chalk stain on his chin.

"Fuck me, Mr. Bollinger."

She said it in the same tone that she might use to request a pint of chocolate milk or a number two pencil. Bollinger backed up slightly and looked at Nina. Had he heard her correctly? The classroom was empty and silent except for the hum of the wall clock that whirred in the background. In his fantasies Nina had been a little frightened—wanting, but tentative. In his imaginary world, tainted by modern fiction and nineteenth century poetry, it had taken all of his soothing charms to maneuver her onto his desk and pierce her as only he really could.

Now here she was, reclining on his simulated wood grain workstation, her skirt hiked up and her index finger deep in her mouth. When she took it out it glistened with wetness, and she stroked at herself with one hand while motioning him over with the other. Quickly finding her rhythm she started to pick up speed on the pile of manila folders that covered what used to be Mr. Bollinger's domain but was now most decidedly hers.

Under the circumstances, Nina was indeed willing to fuck Mr. Bollinger, but given the choice between that and self-gratification it was no contest. She looked better than he did, she smelled better than he did, and she even lied better than he did. For Nina West, masturbation was sex with someone that she both loved and respected, someone who couldn't necessarily spell clitoris, but could actually define it.

Nina placed her free hand under her shirt and began to play herself like a warm bass fiddle. Her head swam with the realization that if Bollinger didn't get started soon she might miss the opening credits of Doctor's Hospice. That was the part where Doctors Tanner and Whiteside and their devoted Nurse Twilley are shown building the practice from a storefront operation to the thriving megalopolis of medicine that gave the longest running daytime show in television history its name.

Two green eyes locked on the English teacher, now hopelessly nervous and confused. Mr. Bollinger felt himself about to faint as his forbidden fantasy began to turn into Nina's own version of forbidden reality.

"Uh…Miss West, I…"

Suddenly the classroom door opened and bald, terminally constipated Vice Principal Carl Swanson entered the room with a pad of pink detention slips and a ballpoint pen. Swanny, as he was known behind his back, had joined the Hare Krishnas in his youth and still bore the trademark shorn head and glazed look that he'd earned annoying people in airports and bus terminals across the United States and Canada.

He looked quizzically at the girl gyrating on the desk and continued to look at her as he handed the pen to Mr. Bollinger without saying a word. Too frozen with fear to speak, he silently signed the pink slips and handed them back to Swanson. Both men still had their eyes glued to the desk where Nina continued her machinations without missing a beat.

Several minutes went by. Nina fondled herself to a climax swearing loudly when she came. She licked her fingers, put her clothes on and left the room glancing at the clock to make sure that she was still on time. The two men, one middle aged, the other with a whole disappointing life ahead of him looked at each other, then at the floor.

"I'll accept your resignation effective immediately, Bollinger," said Swanson as he left, Nina's scent still dancing in his nostrils.

4

Ancient Arts

WALKING HOME FROM SCHOOL Nina spied a small run-down shop with a faded sign that said "ACUPUNCTURE." She couldn't remember having seen it before, although she passed by this same corner nearly every day. Two young Asian girls were playing hopscotch on the sidewalk in front and as Nina passed one of the girls took her hand and said:

"You will please to follow me."

The shop was dark and smelled like a petting zoo, shelves filled to overflowing with herbs, roots, powders and supplements in dusty old tins. Nina turned to look back at the street, but the other little girl had followed them in and locked the door behind her. Nina hesitated for a moment, then continued to follow the first girl down a pitch- black staircase at the back of the shop. She knew that she should feel afraid, but instead a feeling of tremendous calm enveloped her as she listened to her heart beating slowly in her chest.

At the bottom of the stairs was a small room lit entirely by candle and beyond this room, in the next one, lay a large man on a gurney. The little girl motioned for Nina to stop and put her finger to her lips. As Nina's eyes adjusted to the light she became aware of an elderly crone, hunched over like a sclerotic cotton picker, moving busily about the man in the next room. With a delicacy beyond patience, she was placing tiny needles in his legs, neck and fingers. A contented hum came from the man, the only sign other than his slow steady breathing to indicate that he was still alive.

The old woman's skin was rough and leathery, her breathing slow and labored. She wore a shapeless black skirt beneath a dark woolen shawl and her hair was tied in a loose bun atop her wizened old head. Nina could feel the enormous concentration of the acupuncturist as she continued for several minutes more to place pins in the man's feet and ankles, his chest and his forehead. After a few minutes more it seemed like there wasn't anywhere on the prone man's massive body that wasn't covered with the tiny silver needles. Suddenly, the old woman stopped her ministrations and looked up, sniffing the air like a wolf. She peered through the darkness, directly to where Nina sat and said:

"You are the Dirty Girl, huh?"

Nina stood stock still, unable to move or respond in any way. In the pale underground light of the cellar she saw the woman smile a toothless grin. She pointed a bony finger at Nina and said in her cracked, ancient voice:

"You stink in the sunshine, sister. Yeah. It's in darkness that you glow."

At that the man on the table came out of his trance and began to howl in pain. The little girls instantly disappeared up the stairs and the old woman began to chant something in an otherworldly monotone that increased in volume until she drowned out the tortured patient on the gurney, still screaming, his eyes shining wild with fear. The morbid spell that had enveloped the room evaporated, replaced by a queasy sort of chaos.

"She is the one!" yelled the big man, his massive head almost touching the ceiling and his hairy arms flailing wildly as he relived some long buried trauma lodged in the ooze of what could charitably be called his mind.

Despite his best efforts, the subject was unable to touch the tiny old woman who continued her loud chanting as she very calmly grabbed a handful of needles from off of the counter and began to stab the big man with them until he was covered in thin rivulets of blood.

Just as suddenly as he had begun, the big man stopped screaming and resumed his soothing hum, the blood now flowing freely from a hundred small wounds across his body. A gust of stale wind blew the flickering candles out. In the pitch blackness Nina saw the big man's mouth twist into a grimace that pierced the dark like a dead cat. The old woman lanced each of his bug eyes with two long needles and looked up to where she knew Nina was still staring transfixed.

"Can't live with them, can't live without them, huh? You be careful now, Dirty Girl. When you're all alone it gets lonely."

Nina turned and walked slowly up the stairs that led back to the shop. The front door was open and the two little girls were once again playing on the sidewalk in front. Just as Nina emerged, her eyes dazzled by the brightness of the afternoon, one of the girls fell to the ground and scraped her knee. She bent down to help, and the girl timidly offered her leg up to the stranger like a sacrifice. Nina ran her smooth pink tongue across the girl's open wound and frowned.

Tastes like chicken, she thought.

5

Walk On Paperboy

DOCTOR'S HOSPICE HAD BEEN on for forty-five minutes and only one death and one infidelity had transpired so far. Nina's attention began to wander as one of her little spells came on. Her eyes fixed on a point above the rose patterned wallpaper and once again she was one with the furniture. Sweet nothings caressed her petulant mind.

It was then that a wayward copy of the Highland Oaks News came crashing through the picture window showering the sofa in glass fragments and pretty well making Nina's afternoon. That pregnant silence that occurs whenever a young person does something that they know they shouldn't have done followed. Nina heard a bird sing in a tree and an ice cream truck off in the distance. Then Teddy Boyce rang the doorbell and prepared to face the music.

"Oh God, Nina, I am so sorry, I totally didn't mean it, I totally didn't! I am so busted now, my mom's gonna kill me, she's gonna kill me. I'm so sorry, oh God...are you OK?" he asked realizing for the first time that a thin trickle of blood was flowing down Nina's smooth, white forehead and dripping languidly onto the beige of the living room carpet.

Teddy was twelve years old, big for his age with a permanent cowlick and a semi-permanent pair of corduroy pants. He liked pizza, wiffleball and airplanes in that order. Since getting his paper route three months ago he'd enraged Mrs. Capezzi by running across her herb garden and scared Mr. Haverbeck almost to death on his front porch early one morning, but he'd never done anything like this before. He looked around at the room and at Nina and he thought about the trouble that awaited him when his folks found out.

Teddy was growing fast, that much was true, but he was still shy and his chin started to quaver as he fought the crying jag that was coming on like a toy train wreck. He swallowed hard and looked at Nina again. He was determined not to cry in front of a girl, not even a weird one like Nina West.

Nina stared back at him for a long time, saying nothing. She absently grazed her temple with the fingertips of her left hand and put a finger, damp with blood into her mouth and sucked at it. Now Teddy knew he would cry, it was just a matter of when.

Nina took him by the hand and led him to the couch where she had lain alone a few minutes before. She sank to her knees on the carpet, took down the zipper of his blue corduroys, and put his small penis in her mouth. Teddy wanted to run, but he understood instinctively that this strange experience might mitigate, or was in some way a part of, his inevitable punishment. He looked down and saw the top of Nina's head as it caught the light from the broken window and shone like a black halo.

As her excitement mounted, Nina reached up with both hands and pushed Teddy onto the glass covered couch. His hands shot out to break his fall and a dozen sharp splinters pierced his fingers and then the backs of his legs and bare bottom.

"Owww," he said, sounding his age.

Nina looked up into his eyes, her mouth still full, and saw fear. Twelve-year-old Theodore Mason Boyce hadn't yet attempted coitus, but he had ejaculated all over himself one night in the grips of a 102-degree fever. He hadn't enjoyed it.

Looking around the living room Teddy thought again of all the trouble he was going to get into. He was pretty sure that this was supposed to be fun, but still he wanted to cry. He thought of his mother and how sad she got whenever he came home with his shirt stained or his pants ripped. He wondered if he really was a good person or a bad one and he wondered how anybody really knew the difference anyway.

Nina kept sucking furiously and Teddy's cock was hard now in spite of himself. In fact, it wasn't so much hard as petrified. He thought of his teacher, Miss Havisu and his Cub Scout Den Mother, Mrs. Peoples. Everybody always seemed to find out about the bad things he did, and they were all going to be really disappointed this time. All he really knew in that moment was that he had to get out of this house and away from this girl right away.

He pulled on Nina's hair to make her stop, but she seemed to suck twice as hard, and Teddy thought about his mother again (she was really gonna kill him this time) and all of a sudden he came in Nina's mouth. Instantly, Teddy felt remorse. His ass was bleeding freely from the slivers of glass he'd sat on, and he started to cry. Nina wouldn't stop sucking so he slugged her as hard as he could, and she bit him so passionately that he screamed and ran out of the house, his corduroy pants around his ankles and his entire sexual future defined in one random afternoon.

Doctor's Hospice had ended, and Nina began to watch a daytime talk show on the subject of juvenile delinquency.

Andy was fifteen and smoked PCP, Brett was a budding arsonist and Lola wouldn't go to school anymore.

What these kids need is a job, thought Nina.

6

Down Under

NINA TOOK A SEAT near the back of the room. To the degree that she liked anything at all, she actually liked French class. Mademoiselle Granau had a soft voice that lulled her to sleep after lunchtime and Nina had long ago decided that if she ever went to France, she would hire someone to speak for her.

"Oh shit, is this French class?" asked an unfamiliar voice with a tangy New Zealand accent and a clean white tennis dress on. She picked up her books and shifted in her chair. "I'm supposed to be in Spanish!"

Had the new girl been a local, Nina probably would have dismissed her out of hand as either a preppy, an athlete, or some ghastly combination of the two. Her kiwi patois had won her a second look though, and Nina was vaguely intrigued. She glanced at the girl's notebook and saw the name Monica Baker. For no real reason it made her horny.

"Don't go," she said simply. Monica looked quizzically at Nina and put her books back down on the desk. She'd been in this miserable country for a week and a half, and what she really wanted was a friend. It didn't have to be a best friend, or even a good friend, any sort of human contact would do at this point. Nina, somewhat like a kitten in an aquarium, wanted something else.

After class was over the two of them walked the four blocks to Monica's house. It still felt new and unlived in to Monica and she had cried every night since she'd moved in, but it felt like today might be different. While Nina wasn't exactly nice, she wasn't her little brother, her mum or her dad, and Monica was determined to like her at least for the time being. They spent the afternoon watching television and pointing out all of the soap opera actors they thought were cute. Later, Monica poked her head in the refrigerator and pulled out two beers.

"Care for a cold one?" she asked, popping the tops with a practiced air.

Nina drank some and placed the bottle on the counter. It fizzed up and over the top of the bottle and Monica laughed loudly showing a mouth brimming with straight white teeth. Nina came close to laughing herself, but she checked the impulse and managed a faint smile instead, a hint of shiny metal peeking through her slightly parted lips.

"Oh, those braces are totally tits," said Monica, "I wish I had some."

She took a long pull off of the bottle and smiled. Then she burped, snorted and started laughing again. This time Nina couldn't help it and she joined in. Monica reached out and tickled Nina, who momentarily didn't feel like being snotty anymore. Was this what it felt like to be friends with someone? Nina shuddered internally at the thought.

When the laughter subsided, Monica became very quiet. She looked as deeply into Nina's eyes as she could without giggling. She seemed to be searching for something, and then she turned away again. Just as Nina began to get bored with the whole thing, Monica leaned in and kissed her tentatively on the mouth.

"I used to go to Girl's School," she said by way of explanation, "everybody does it."

Nina didn't care who else did it; she wanted to do it, too. As they slid to the floor, their lips pressed together in a frenzy of lager and bubblegum, Nina had a vision of herself as a little black-haired wallaby returning to the pouch. As the clinch intensified Monica tried to tell her that she hadn't gone much beyond kissing, but Nina had already relieved her of the frilly underthing that matched her cheery little skirt and had zeroed in on her vulva like an Australian homing pigeon.

The lure of down under being what it was, the two fast friends spent the afternoon exploring every nook and cranny of the sparsely furnished house, stopping only when Monica's mother announced her arrival with that eternal question:

"Who wants a little something before dinner?"

The next day, Nina found it even harder than usual to concentrate in French class. As she played with herself under the desk a wad of chewed gum worked its way into her fantasy, and she left the room determined from that moment forward to pretend to learn Spanish instead.

7

Nina West vs. the Girl Scouts of America

Highland Oaks High School, in cooperation with Highland Oaks Junior High School, ran a tutoring program where bright students helped younger peers with their studies. Since it was worth two credits instead of the one that most classes were, Nina swallowed her distaste for both charity and the young and volunteered.

When a mechanized bell tolled the end of classes for the day, Nina found herself wandering aimlessly around the emptying corridors of HOJHS. Passing the gym, she became enchanted by the site of a troupe of green clad fairies sitting cross-legged on the shiny wooden floor. Their scrubbed, attentive faces were turned upward, carefully absorbing instructions from an overgrown sprite that addressed them from behind a Formica table laden with boxes.

As she came closer, she realized that the boxes contained cookies, Girl Scout cookies to be precise, and she wanted some. Since nature had blessed Nina with a perfect physique and a rapid metabolism, she felt that it was her duty to eat as much unhealthy food as she could. She considered it a tribute to her less fortunate peers who spent most of their time agonizing over calories and skin problems or vomiting clandestinely in the girl's bathroom. Nina queued up behind two chubby young Scouts and when she got to the front of the line she was handed two boxes each of Mint Munchaways, Peanut Butter Pinwheels and Shortbread Shorties.

She almost smiled at the Scoutmaster who said:

"Be sure to wear your uniform next time, dear."

Out in the parking lot, Nina began to tear into a box of Shorties and fantasize about a tall glass of milk to go with it. The unmistakable sound of the package being opened stirred some primordial impulse in the green clad gaggle of girls behind her. Witnessing this heresy, they turned on her as savagely as a badger in a petting zoo.

"Like, what are you doing?" asked Amy Francis, whose uniform was festooned with so many merit badges it almost made her look like she had breasts. "You still have to pay for them, even if you just, like, pig out on them all by yourself."

"The idea," said Carolyn Trow, dedicated to the cause since the Brownies, "is to sell the cookies to other people, so that the Girl Scouts can donate the money to charities like the Children's Hospital and Muscular Dystrophy. Duh!"

Nina was on the verge of telling these self-important little drones to eat a bag of shit when she hit upon a better plan. She began limping and dragging her left foot behind her as she continued munching on. Three blocks from school, with best friends Amy and Carolyn following, whispering, and pointing, Nina stumbled and fell hard onto the sidewalk.

"Oh my God," yelled the Scouts in unison.

Amy added the obligatory, "Are you, like, OK?" as the pair rushed to assist Nina from up off the sidewalk. She summoned a look of abject misery, her orbs filled with glycerin tears, as she looked into the anxious eyes of Amy and Carolyn.

"It's the thrombosis," she said, "sometimes it's hard to walk and stuff. I'm sorry, I'll be OK."

The Scouts looked at each other with grim determination. This was just the type of thing their organization had been preparing them for since the second grade. A fellow student, a plainclothes Scout no less, was in need, and they were prepared to help in any way that they could. Nina assured them that she was fine, walked a few steps and sank to the ground again, her knees giving way beneath her. Amy and Carolyn insisted on walking her home as Nina resisted, then relented.

Back on her home turf, she searched the medicine cabinet in her parent's bathroom for sleeping pills. She crumbled up ten of the blue ones and returned to the kitchen where she mixed them into a pitcher of chocolate milk. She put the pitcher on a platter with some cookies and returned to the living room where Amy and Carolyn were watching the closing minutes of Doctor's Hospice.

"Thanks, you guys. It was so nice of you to walk me home and stuff. Sometimes with the phlebitis, the gingivitis, the whooping cough…" here she dissolved into a choking spasm, "it really gets lonely."

"You should stick with the Scouts," said Carolyn who needed to sign up three more girls to qualify for yet another merit badge. "It's a great way to meet people and make new friends while serving the community."

Nina considered the concept of serving the community as she refilled the girls rapidly emptying milk glasses. She was glad that her mother favored a popular new sedative, Prourinol, that not only put one to sleep, but had the added effect of cleansing one's short-term memory and replacing it with a sort of vague mind-numbing dread about what one might have done while under its influence. Scenes from the next episode of Doctor's Hospice played as several long minutes went by. Amy yawned and excused herself. Carolyn sank further into the couch and her eyes began to flutter into submission.

Nina waited until Carolyn's prepubescent chest began to

rhythmically rise and fall before she headed to the bathroom to find Amy on the white tile floor gently snoring under the influence of the pills. The girl looked just like an annoying little angel.

Besides the precious creatures themselves, who can say what preteen girls dream about in the twilight realm of adult prescriptions? Unicorns, pixies, puppy dogs, movie stars, race-car drivers, pin up heartthrobs, lumberjacks, grandma's preserves, pesky li'l brothers? Although it had only been three years since she'd been there herself, Nina didn't care to remember.

She dragged them both to the living room and removed their uniforms, making sure to leave their brown merit sashes in the foreground. Then she went to her father's closet and removed his Nikon camera. Nina had enjoyed photography ever since reading that primitive tribes thought the process robbed natives of their very souls. She draped the girls over, under and around each other, moving constantly as she clicked the shots to make the Scouts appear both conscious and mobile.

When an entire roll of innuendo had been shot, she dressed them again and dragged them out into the street. The sun hung low in the sky when the Scouts came to, surrounded by boxes of half-eaten cookies and the inescapable feeling that something was very wrong indeed.

Nina decided that the time was ripe for her to penetrate that font of misinformation, the Internet. Within days the pictures had been posted on a number of websites including HornyScouts.com, much to the delight of the online pederast community.

Be prepared, thought Nina, wondering why the Girl Scouts couldn't get a motto of their own.

8

Opportunity Knocks

Anton Gregory had only been a security guard at Highland Oaks High for two weeks when he handed the pink note to Miss Hardy. A. G., as his boys called him, hadn't quite finished high school himself, but he had (after time served for Petty Theft and a Failure to Appear) received his Equivalency Degree. His mother had been so proud that she had taken the day off from work to be with her only son on his special day, even though the diploma was mailed to him, and he wasn't invited to the graduation ceremony. Here on the other side of the tracks the classroom hushed as he entered, bracing for the name that would be called out and sent down the long dark hallway of the soul that is detention.

"Nina West, the vice-principal would like to see you in his office please."

Nina rose and sauntered slowly up the rows of wooden desks and chairs. As always, she felt the stares from boys still struggling with impending manhood and the girls still struggling with just about everything else. Nina didn't like high school boys very much, but she had even less use for their female counterparts. Was there a difference between not having any friends and not wanting any?

Walking the mud colored halls of Highland Oaks she'd always felt like an alien, both illegal and from outer space. Now as she headed toward the office, she felt that familiar fog on the corners of her brain, like a black velvet sheet over her wandering thoughts. She was glad to be afflicted with only a mild form of epilepsy and not the 'rolling-on-the-ground-with-a-spoon-in-your-mouth' variety. That would have been too much work. Sometimes when the diverting little fits would come on, she would see her short life pass before her eyes, like an old cartoon on a dirty bed sheet, and some days she enjoyed the show more than others.

Nina had never been summoned to the office before, but she recognized Mr. Shaffner from photographs that she'd tried to ignore in the yearbook. He rose to his feet when he saw her and motioned somberly to a white plastic chair in front of his desk. Had he been an armed guard at a concentration camp or a sheriff who evicted old people from their homes he might have felt badly about his job, but to his way of thinking vice-principal Vince Shaffner was just doing what needed to be done to educate our nation's most precious resource, its youngsters. There was no nobler calling, no duty more sacred than that and although he was an administrator and not a teacher per se, by studying him carefully one could perhaps learn what not to do with the gift of existence.

"Nina, sit down. I have something very difficult to say and before I go on I want you to know that all of us here at Highland Oaks are behind you one hundred percent, we really are."

Nina's face remained impassive as she wondered fleetingly if this balding, insignificant man wanted to fuck her. She decided that he did, and she became within the span of one half second disgusted and titillated and then disgusted again by the prospect.

"There isn't any easy way to say this, so I'm just going to come right out with it. Your parents were passengers on an airplane that went down near Sioux Falls this morning.

They both died instantly. A representative of their estate will contact you later this afternoon with more details, and our social worker Mrs. Fromash would like to speak with you after we finish here. Nina, if there's anything we can do, please don't hesitate to ask."

After an uncomfortable interval Nina stood up and walked out of the room, ignoring Shaffner's parting words, whatever they were. She went to her locker and spun the combination lock aimlessly. Then she looked around at the metallic brown hallway and headed out the weathered wooden doors and down the concrete steps of Highland Oaks High School for the very last time.

Euphoria began to play around the edges of her mind. Just like that, she was free of the parents who had bored her; free of the school that could teach her nothing. The inheritance would be substantial. She was an only child, the daughter of only children. Even her grandparents were dead and gone with their pinching and fussing and medicine smells. There was no one left but her.

It occurred to Nina that in this life, unless you needed sex, it really was better to be alone. In fact, sometimes when you were alone even the sex was better. In the past when she had watched television or gone to the movies or stayed up late listening to old songs on the radio Nina had wondered how some people could get so emotional about things. They screamed, sang, fought, apologized, even dropped to their knees and begged for mercy or a job that they hated anyway. Seeing them like that always made her want to switch species.

Nina knew that that corner of herself set aside for love and hate, for infatuation and longing, for jealousy and deceit just didn't exist. When she was younger, she had wondered what was wrong with her, but as she grew she realized, with that abstract certainty that governs the workings of every mind, that she was lucky to be free of want and still so full of desire.

"I told them I didn't need a sitter," she thought, and promptly forgot what her parents had looked like.

9

Forgive Me Father

NINA WANDERED THROUGH TOWN in the middle of the day, intoxicated with the freedom that had been loosed upon her. She could do anything that she liked now. She wanted a cigarette but refused to smoke in front of anyone else for fear of being seen as dependent on anything.

Down the block the imposing façade of Immaculate Conception Church loomed over downtown Highland Oaks. After a lifetime spent studiously avoiding all things religious it suddenly seemed like the most natural thing in the world to walk through its big iron doors and see how the other half lived. That is, if you called that living.

Nina took a seat by the back and watched as half a dozen old women prayed so fervently that she could almost believe there was someone listening. Nina stared at the statue of the Virgin Mary until it began to cry. At first the tears fell slowly from the smooth alabaster face, but before long thick wet rivulets ran down the length of the icon and began to puddle on the floor. Mrs. Minarini was the first to see the vision, which brought her to her stubby varicose feet loudly proclaiming a miracle. Mrs. Ronan and her daughter-in-law Terry Noonan leapt to their feet as well, setting off a stampede of undiluted Catholic womanhood that stopped abruptly at the foot of the weeping statue.

Nina crossed to the other side of the big open church hall. She had seen people coming and going from a small room partitioned off to the side and she was curious about what was going on back there. Inside she saw a latticework window and the outline of an imposing man on the other side. At first glance he appeared too fat to sleep with, but she was willing to modify her position if circumstances changed.

"Come in my dear, don't be bashful."

Nina knelt uncomfortably in front of the little window and waited. The air was stale and tasted faintly of moth-balls and old wine. Dust motes blew across the floor as the priest waited for her to break the silence, but she never did.

"How long has it been since your last confession?"

"This is my first time," she said, aware that this was the first time she had ever used that particular phrase before.

"And what would you like to share with me today?"

Nina thought of Larry West, of Teddy Boyce and Mr. Bollinger. She thought of lesbians and acupuncture, of alcohol, tobacco, and firearms. She thought of her parents and how they were now food for the worms and weevils in a glorious, empty afterlife.

"Nothing, really."

"Come now, you needn't be afraid. Your secrets are safe with me, I've heard all kinds of things in this room, and I promise you, anything that you say here will stay between the two of us. Open up, child, it'll do your heart good."

Nina considered this advice and at that moment she almost felt like taking it. It might make her feel better to confide in this harmless old man. He seemed to want nothing more from her than to ease her tortured soul as it withered under the sad gaze of the Lord on his Cross. And even though she wasn't Catholic, wasn't even religious by nature, there had to be something to this God business, if only because so many people had believed in it for so long. Ruminating thus, she prepared to bare her putrefying conscience to this shadow man in his private booth communing with heaven. Then just as abruptly she reconsidered and screamed as loudly as she could:

"RAPE! HELP, HE'S TRYING TO RAPE ME!"

Nina ran screaming from the confessional. Father Burgoine emerged just as she reached the army of supplicants, now a dozen old women strong, in front of the statue. She collapsed in the warm embrace of black nylons and orthopedic shoes as the ladies turned their gaze on the priest who, as fate would have it, the parishioners had never really liked anyway. The general consensus among the faithful was that his modern airs and newfangled notions about things were bound to get him into trouble someday. Terry Noonan said:

"The Blessed Mother knew what you were up to, Father, and she cried for us all to see."

"This girl is disturbed, ladies, she needs help…"

"Not your kind of help, Father. You've profaned this place, you've even made the Virgin weep, but you'll not get your hands on this girl except over our dead bodies."

Nina considered what Terry Noonan's body would look like dead and decided that it wasn't much worse than the semi animated version that stood self-righteously before her now, spewing flecks of spittle from the corners of her parched old lips. The priest addressed Nina directly:

"My dear, you must tell the truth. Your soul depends on it."

Now it was Mrs. Minarini that piped up in Nina's defense. She had heard Burgoine's highfalutin talk before, had read his letters to the editor and his missives to the Holy See, and she wasn't impressed. If it wasn't peace marches in Venezuela, or gays in the military, it was abortions on demand and alcoholics in the Rectory.

"Don't you dare threaten this poor girl again, Father. You're the one that seems to have a problem with the Truth."

Nina suddenly grew very tired of the church and its inhabitants. Even maliciously toying with them was an exercise in futility. Despite their superficial differences all of these glorified pagans had one thing in common—they cared, and therefore they were doomed. She looked at the statue of the Virgin, which winked at her in reply.

"I hate this place, and I hate all of you," said Nina, and here she addressed Father Burgoine, "especially you, you old pervert."

She turned and strolled out through the big iron doors of the church, her head held high, her chunky heels clattering down the staircase outside. The old ladies looked accusingly at Father Thaddeus Jude Burgoine who felt lost, humbled and forsaken as his morning wish to be more like Christ began to take shape in a way that he hadn't dreamed possible.

The statue of the Virgin Mary blew Her nose and silently prayed for a tissue.

10

The Mile High School

NATHAN BUNCH OPERATED A motorized cart at James K. Polk International Airport for passengers who couldn't get around without assistance. All of the illegal immigrants who had formerly worked there had been fired for security reasons and African-Americans were now, for the first time ever, considered a safer hyphenate. Nathan had driven old folks, quadriplegics, terminal patients, and the blind to their respective gates for three years now and he'd never done so without advance confirmation from an air carrier stipulating who was to go where and when. That was how the job was done, and he liked it that way.

But Nina West had caught his eye as she walked through the sliding glass doors of entrance 44B and before Nathan knew it, he had asked what gate she was headed for, loaded her bags onto the cart and hatched a fantasy that had made his loins strain against the coarse fabric of his blue denim work pants. The fantasy ended abruptly as she disembarked and handed him a meager tip without smiling.

The rich bitches always look like they're going to a funeral, he thought.

At the gate stood a wisp of a man in a sleeveless sweater and yellow pants whose sexual orientation made him immune to Nina's charms. As he scrutinized her high school ID a grimace spread over his cleanly shaven face.

"I'm sorry, I'll need to get my supervisor to approve this, hang on just a minute, Miss West."

Fortunately for Nina, Captain Duncan McNeil chose that moment to pass by in his pressed blue uniform, Ray Bans glinting in the reflected light from his shoes. McNeil quickly sized up the situation, smiled broadly and clapped the flight attendant so hard on the back that he nearly collapsed, gasping for air and feeling three bags of dry roasted peanuts near the top of his throat. "I'll take control of this young lady in loco parentis, my friend. Please come with me, Miss," he said, extending his elbow gallantly and sweeping her down the dingy tangerine jet way toward the waiting plane, inwardly winking at whatever deity supplies aging Lotharios with fresh meat.

The next few minutes were a whirlwind of activity. Nina sat quietly in a fold out chair in the cockpit as the Captain, his copilot and three different stewardesses ran through their take off sequence and gave her looks ranging from quizzical to amused to the full on Evil Eye. This came from flight attendant Melanie Crane, McNeil's now forgotten conquest of last week. When they were done with the take-off sequence, a nod and a gesture sent the co-pilot out to check cabin pressure.

As the plane pierced an azure sky, the Captain sat Nina roughly on his knee and they began petting heavily. Contrary to her usual attitude of total indifference, Nina decided in a fit of adolescent emotion to abandon herself completely to the whims of her partner this time. Of course, that was just fine by Duncan McNeil.

In college McNeil had played football and then, under doctor's orders, had switched to fencing where he had excelled, ultimately gaining a spot as an alternate on the US Olympic Team. As an Air Force Colonel, he'd performed heroically in battle over the arid deserts of Kuwait and the stifling streets of Mogadishu. He knew the ins and outs of hedge funds, Moroccan restaurants, and Italian sports cars as well as the proper booze to mixer ratios in a Gibson, a Mojito and even a vintage Harvey Wallbanger. Compared to his past accomplishments, making this little cupcake squeal was going to be like a walk in the park.

McNeil's technique was classic, his timing impeccable, and his form superb. For her part, Nina was glad to have someone else take the reins for a change. And the Captain, with his age, good looks, and spiffy uniform, fulfilled quite a few fantasies that her conquests back in Highland Oaks had never even approached.

"You like it when I do you like that, baby?" McNeil asked semi- rhetorically, trying to get a glimpse of himself in the small circular mirror that hung on the back of the cockpit door.

Nina considered the question. Of course, she liked it, she'd have to be paralyzed not to. Being a teenage girl, Nina's experiences with foreplay were minimal. She just assumed that like everything else she was better at it than the rest of the human race, and before she knew it Duncan Jr. had in-filtrated her inner sanctum like a cold knife through warm butter. Now, feeling McNeil's tan, athletic penis inside of her she could also feel his point. Sex was always good; it was other people that were bad.

The pilot looked at his newest conquest, still awaiting the answer to his pawed, sweaty inquiry.

"Yes," she said inscrutably, adding nothing and causing McNeil, amped on caffeine, Rogaine, and anabolic steroids, to pump at her that much harder.

She'd like it all right, on that point he was bound and determined. By the time he was through with her he'd have her begging for it. McNeil flipped Nina out of his chair and onto the floor of the cramped cockpit, his hardness never flagging for an instant. And she could now smell the real him, beyond the European aftershave and fabric softener and yes, she enjoyed it tremendously. He certainly knew what he was doing, that was for sure. That is, until he started talking again.

"I'm gonna do you like you want, baby, just like you want. Tell me how you like it, how you want it in your sweet little…"

Nina did want it, and she knew that she wanted it. What's more, she knew that he knew that she wanted it. The thing was; he wanted her to say it. And that she didn't want.

Nina was impressed with the chiseled musculature, the massive hair carpeted chest, the leathery skin, but something about his total mastery of the environment, including now Nina herself, was more than she could bear. As Nina looked up and beyond the Captain's broad shoulders, she saw the public address intercom switch and she flipped it to the "ON" position.

"Oh, yeah, you know you want it baby, say it, say it!"

This time Nina had no trouble expounding at length on the wonderful fucking that Captain Duncan McNeil was giving her. She screamed it and moaned it, she gurgled and sighed it, she begged and pleaded and yelled and swore it, until the Captain sent a whole besunglassed platoon of eager spermatozoa screeching toward her ovaries determined to plant the red flag of passion thereon.

Listening spellbound in the cabin of the wide-bodied jet the more worldly passengers were highly entertained. Others thought the display of amplified verbal sexuality in poor taste, but just one of those things that happened sometimes, like sunspots or spontaneous combustion. The Carmelite nuns on their way to a conclave in Monterey, however, were mortified enough for the entire plane. And the Mormon elders preparing to connect for their flight to Salt Lake City weren't very happy either, once it had been established that the pair were unmarried and the pilot old enough to be the girl's…well, her uncle at the very least.

Nina's ululations had drowned out the sound of the co-pilot and crew pounding on the cockpit door, which was locked for security reasons. Basking in the afterglow, already fantasizing about a Cuban cigar the size of a baby's leg, McNeil finally heard the frantic knocking, and then the echo of his own voice booming through the cabin as he remarked, "keep your fucking shirt on." Realizing the implications of this latest mile high adventure McNeil's ruddy complexion whitened and even proud Duncan Jr. shriveled in a rush of recirculated air.

Captain Duncan McNeil, often described as the man who had everything, got more than he had bargained for from his tryst with young Nina West. After several hours of questioning by officials highly placed at the airline and the FAA, it was agreed that the pilot should be removed from active duty without pay for the remainder of his contract and permanently prohibited from flying for any licensed air carrier in the United States and its Protectorates. When it was further determined that the minor in question was an orphan and not inclined to sue or press charges, Nina agreed to a settlement which included free first-class airfare for the rest of her natural life and the sum of $35,000, a figure that she had heard quoted during the in-flight movie *Spy Kids 5: Operation Rising*.

11

San Narcisso

NINA DECIDED TO GO to San Francisco. She had heard that it was interesting, but after walking up and down the ancient ruins of Haight Street twice now she wasn't so sure. It had been the most tedious twenty minutes she'd spent since her parents' memorial service in Laramie, Wyoming. Her father's last wish was to have his ashes and those of his wife scattered over the high plains and to have the wrinkled pastor of his youth say a few words at the funeral. Like any really unfortunate date, no one had come.

"Excuse me, would you like to sign this petition to stop the devastation of our National Parklands?"

Nina surveyed the object in front of her. Tall, muscular, earnest, good teeth, kind of a hippie; but he'd have to do. She remembered hearing someone say once that politics makes strange bedfellows, so she smoothed her hair over one ear, ran her tongue over her lips quickly and looked him full in the face.

"I think I would like that."

Jeremy Cobb didn't wake that morning thinking that he would be treated to lunch and a long soak in the Jacuzzi at the Westin St. Francis Hotel before enjoying sex on clean white sheets with an obscenely high thread count, but neither did he feel undeserving of such treatment. After all, a few redwoods were still standing and that was in some small way due to the efforts of people like him. This was probably just Mother Earth in one of her many guises thanking him for making the world a better place. Jeremy's cellular phone rang twice, but he made no move to answer it.

"Is that your girlfriend?" asked Nina, reaching over him quickly and answering the phone before he could reply.

"Hello...no, you have the right number. This is Nina West, I'm supervising Jeremy today and he asked me to mind his phone while he canvasses door to door."

Jeremy's heart fluttered, while Nina sat listening and absently stroking at herself. A mind-wandering bout of epilepsy threatened to well up in the back of her mind, but she willed it away. She suddenly felt that Jeremy's girlfriend might be very interesting, or at the very least more interesting than Jeremy. Someone less interesting than Jeremy was inconceivable.

"I'll be sure and give him the message Nadine, he's been working awfully hard today... Well, would you like to meet us for dinner later, it really would be my pleasure? It's no trouble at all, really...uh, huh...Market and Powell at seven-thirty is perfect, we'll see you then."

Jeremy was not happy with this new development. Nadine was open-minded when it came to issues of global trade or the ozone layer, but she could be downright old-fashioned when it came to stuff like this. And as hot as Nina was, she was also more than a little bit creepy. He'd noticed too late that her shoes were made from dead cow and her coat once hunted the dusty African savanna looking for antelope.

"Uh, I better take off now..."

"Nonsense, Jeremy, we have a dinner date with your Nadine. She sounds like a fascinating person."

Nadine Reynolds was full, round, and healthy, the type of girl for whom the phrase childbearing hips was coined.

She dressed much like Jeremy, but her blue jeans were clean, and her shirt had been ironed and her hair was tied back in a loose ponytail that smelled faintly of vanilla. A believer by nature she had faith in the transformative power of grass-roots activism, Chinese astrology and Jeremy's very average guitar playing among other things. She could also make short work of a good meal if the opportunity presented itself.

"Have another glass of wine, Nadine, it's organic."

Nadine didn't need to be asked again. She had made short work of her tortellini in a shiitake mushroom sauce, downing two glasses of white wine in the process, and she felt good. Nina was aloof but nice enough. Jeremy seemed preoccupied as usual, but tonight she wasn't having it. Tonight, the red-woods would just have to fend for themselves because Nadine wanted to have a little fun for a change.

"Nina, you seem like the type of person that enjoys a good poem."

Jeremy felt his heart sink. He was afraid that this was going to happen. Every time Nadine got drunk, she and her art school friends went through the same quasi-collegiate ritual. First, they would bore him to tears with some sort of Performance (he refused to call it) Art—perhaps a poem, a story, if they were feeling expansive maybe a monologue or two. Then they would all drink themselves silly and start frowning at him, only to end the evening in a hail of ex-istential angst or armchair radical political discourse he didn't care which. Nadine would ignore him until his sulk-ing made her uncomfortable and they staggered home, not speaking.

"There's a reading tonight at Sufficient Grounds and afterward we're going to sit on the roof with a few of my friends. There are some great people that hang out there. Jer-emy hates it, but it seems like it might be your kind of thing."

"As long as Jeremy hates it, I'm game," said Nina, enjoying the sight of Jeremy squirming as she rubbed the outline of his groin under the white linen tablecloth.

12

Poetry in Motion

THE SUFFICIENT GROUNDS COFFEE house nestled in the first floor of an imposing old Victorian house in a nondescript area of San Francisco. The neighborhood had been largely black, or as no one ever said, African American, until real estate speculation had rendered it uninhabitable to those whose contract with America had expired.

"What have you got?" asked Nina, hoping to infuriate the tattooed, pierced and bedreadlocked hermaphrodite behind the counter of the Sufficient Grounds coffeehouse.

By way of answer, it gestured to a sign on the wall, a painstakingly crafted mocha Magna Carta written in colored chalk, featuring every conceivable beverage containing coffee beans. Nina enjoyed her cup as much as the next, provided the next wasn't in Alcoholics Anonymous or a Teamster, but for some reason the modern bohemian atmosphere of this place had set her teeth on edge from the moment she had walked in.

I'll have a triple Latte Formosa with a hint of anisette, whipped cream, and a sprinkle of cinnamon. Then I want you to pour it down your shirt and start crying big, wet crocodile tears you fat tart, she thought, as she asked for a regular no cream, no sugar.

On the small wooden stage at the back of the dining area a young man with an earnest expression and an acoustic guitar prepared to entertain the small crowd who had come to participate in what was commonly known as Open Mic Night. This was a weekly event where would-be performers were given the chance to strut their stuff before a real, live, nonpaying audience. Although the talent wasn't generally of a very high caliber, everyone present was either white, in college, or both so one's chances of getting booed offstage and pelted with rotten fruit, however deserving one might be of such treatment, were very low indeed.

The young man swiped at his guitar, and it responded with a chord that could only be described as unpleasant. The voice that issued from his reefer-coated throat was no better. The song meandered tunelessly, and Nina began to get frustrated. As she listened further and took in more of her surroundings, she got more frustrated and then still more frustrated until she walked up to where a massive lump of woman sat with a clipboard by the side of the stage.

"How much longer does this go on?" Nina asked, in a voice that suggested she'd rather that it didn't. The woman pushed the clipboard and a pen toward her.

"If you can do better, you're welcome to try," she said, in a voice that suggested she'd rather Nina didn't. Nina looked at the clipboard, then at the stage, then back to the thing behind the counter, at Jeremy and Nadine and their friends and finally back at the enormous object who sat before her. She wrote down the name Melody Frobusher and returned to her seat.

With growing bemusement, she sat through an indignant recitation on Nicaragua and one on Kurdistan, then through a juggler and a knife swallower and a woman who could imitate over three dozen bird calls. She heard two lesbians duet on an old Indigo Girls song and witnessed a man miming the death of the rainforest and then it was her turn. She walked to the stage in her high heels and surveyed the crowd. To say that they were unattractive was to put it mildly. Although she knew it was unfair, Nina blamed higher education for this whole sorry scene. If this were indeed the future seated before her then maybe we should just give up now and invite the North Koreans to take whatever they wanted before it was too late.

"My name is Melody Frobusher," she began, and quizzical looks ricocheted around Jeremy and Nadine's table. Their attention was now full and undivided and aimed toward the tiny stage, "and I'd like to read a poem for you."

Nina had neither read nor written a poem before in her entire life, but she didn't think it would be very hard and there seemed to be no time like the present to attempt it. She cleared her throat and looked out at the crowd again. Then she looked directly at Jeremy and ran her tongue over her lips.

"The Giant Redwood," she began:

"So big and bold with shriveled sacs beneath its sturdy,
brainless trunk;
I hunger briefly for your hippie rod,
your beggar's banquet;
Stranded in a Berkeley of the soul,
you asking change receive erection, elation;
Mother Earth waits patiently at home, feeding;
Ungainly, like five pounds of sunflowers
in a three-pound balloon;
The scent of patchouli and brown pot,
corduroys stiff with eco-friendly detergent;
Your middle button missing,
underwear a musty gray stain beneath;
A chance encounter I'll always regret,

no sunshine penetrates the dullness
of your Rainforest mind,
like dead geese in a fern bar, primordial, retarded;
In stinking tye-dye you rise from my mattress
undeserving, Mother Earth calls to check up on you,
while you lie, like moss on the planet's floor;
I who tasted blandly of your wrinkled head,
bought you dinner,
I whom you just met this afternoon…"

At no time during the whole recitation did her eyes leave Jeremy's, even when Nadine hauled off and smacked him hard, right in the nose ring, blood spiking the tepid chamomile tea that sat untouched in front of him. Jeremy hated violence, there had to be a better way. Nadine, however, was prepared to inflict enough damage on him to make up for Jeremy's daily mood swings, his knack for peeing on the floor in front of the toilet, the three months of free rent that he had promised to repay just as soon as he could, and the thirty-some-odd macrobiotic dinners she'd cooked for him since they'd been living together which now felt like forever.

Since fights (except those of the intellectual variety or concerning the guilt or innocence of this or that Maoist revolutionary) were very uncommon at Sufficient Grounds, there was no bouncer to save Jeremy from his better two-thirds. Nadine hit him yet again as he slumped in his chair, sending the table clattering to the floor in a jumble of glass, liquid and gluten-free snacks. The hefty talent coordinator tried to rise quickly from her chair by the stage to see what the fuss was about, but the effort made her face flush and her head spin. She also failed to notice that her genuine Patagonian rain poncho had gotten caught beneath her chair and she fell heavily to the floor with a great bellow of misery.

Jeremy tried as best he could to shield his head from the surprisingly hearty Birkenstock sandals that seemed to assault him from every direction at once. Nina left the stage unnoticed and strolled out the door, nicking a stray macaroon from under a plastic case on the bar in the confusion and hailing a cab in the gray rain outside.

"Where to, Miss?" asked Mujabir, a recent immigrant from Pakistan whose broad smile showed a mouth full of cracked and rotten teeth.

His radio was tuned to a foreign language station and the cab smelled of incense, cigarettes and wet dog. She looked at the picture of her driver on his hack's license and noted the wrinkles by his eyes that made him appear to be laughing and sobbing at the same time.

"Two roads diverged in a yellow wood," thought Nina and settled back in her seat.

13

Suffer the Ignorant

"I'LL HAVE A PACK of Starburst, the SweeTARTS and some Doublemint gum," Nina said to Nadir Abbas.

His look of complete bewilderment was tempered with a kind of inward tranquility that came from years of quiet contemplation and a profound lack of imagination. Nadir had immigrated to the United States and settled in San Francisco because his family had felt that would be best for their well-meaning, intelligent, but rather inept son. Educated as a particle physicist in his native land he was almost equal to the task of selling unhealthy snack foods to America's poor and indigent, but not quite.

"Doublemint, not Spearmint", Nina said, amazed as always that even the simplest things always had to be hard.

As she turned to leave, two men with stockings over their faces entered the liquor store handguns drawn. Nina received a hard smack to her left cheek that sent her flying into a quavering pyramid of Dinty Moore beef stew cans that clattered to the ground taking her with them. She might have lost consciousness, but only for a moment and it wasn't half bad.

"I am very poor," said Nadir, "very, very poor."

He opened the cash register to show the thieves just how poor he was, but they weren't interested. To show the true depth of their disinterest, one of the men struck him on the jaw with the butt of his gun and Nadir slumped, unconscious and miserable to the floor of his shop. The two men immediately made their way to the back of the store, where they knew the shopkeeper's safe hung behind a framed portrait of the Prophet.

"Let's blow this shit!" said the taller of the masked men, Chuy Quintero, to his shorter accomplice Wayne Wygant.

The pair had first met in the San Francisco County Jail. It was a structure that bore little similarity to the Coit Tower or Golden Gate Bridge, but many more people visited it each year, looking for they knew not what. Wayne had waded into a group of Mexicans stomping what he was sure was a fellow Aryan Brother. When the dust had cleared and it was revealed that the victim was actually another Mexican, who couldn't speak Spanish and had an enormous Slayer tattoo on his forehead, the two became fast friends. They celebrated their release by getting drunk, shaving their heads and buying two loaded weapons from Chuy's cousin Jaime.

Jaime, who had lost the use of his legs in a drive by shooting, had also supplied the stick-up men with plastic explosives to blow the safe that hung in the back of a liquor store that he knew of across town. He had explained that the set up was perfect because the place was usually empty, and the dreamy eyed owner was so oblivious that local ten-year-olds routinely beat him out of candy, snacks and comics.

"Even you two dipshits couldn't miss," he had said. And after just four hours of freedom, Wayne and Chuy could hardly believe their luck.

Nina remained on the floor surrounded by canned goods and kept quiet. She wanted to get up and run, but she didn't want to get shot, smacked, or molested by these unpredictable urban misfits. Nadir was still behind the counter, bleeding freely and dreaming dreams of plump young girls in filmy harem costumes. Outside, traffic blew by in the hot dusty street. A drunk shook his fist at the wheezing exhaust pipes of a passing car that didn't care if he was breathing or not.

In the back of the shop the would-be safecrackers struggled with the plastic explosives. Chuy and Wayne had had a few shots of tequila to calm their nerves before the heist. Then they'd gotten some airplane glue and a can of rug cleaner and now Chuy couldn't remember what Jaime had told him about how much of the explosives to use. He figured "better safe than sorry" and just stuffed the whole wad by the metal handle that jutted out like a middle finger from the front of the locked metal box.

The explosion was deafening. Nadir Abbas awoke from his reverie sure that he was dead and resolved to stay behind the counter until Allah himself told him that it was all right to move again. Nina got up and headed for the door, ambivalent now at the prospect of continued survival. A deep groan from the back room made her turn around in the doorway of the liquor store. Another groan convinced her that they couldn't do her any more harm than they had already done to themselves.

The grisly tableau in the back of the store reminded Nina of a documentary she'd seen on the History Channel once about Hitler's Bunker. Chuy Quintero lay dead, his entire head blown off by the force of the blast. Wayne Wygant, always a day late and three bucks short, still clung to life like a pawn surrounded by kings, queens, and bishops eager to end the charade once and for all. In his death throes, his head bleeding freely, his tongue lolling out of his head he spied Nina and thought that a dark angel had come to escort him personally to the Great Beyond. He reached out with what was left of his right hand.

Nina realized that she was out of danger and resolved to get back into it as quickly as possible. She reached into Wayne Wygant's pants and extracted his penis, a rather large and healthy specimen, his only source of pride in a life that mainly consisted of doing stupid things and getting caught for them. Nina began to stroke Wayne, all the while looking in his eyes as if to say, 'I understand.' She didn't though. She could no more understand the mind of a loser than how to fix a jet engine or perform a root canal.

No matter. As she jerked he got harder, as even a man in his last shuddering spasms of life will do when confronted with an attractive woman and an unprovoked sex act. He exhaled, smiled, gurgled pathetically—and when he came, he went.

Nina reached into the safe that swung open with a satisfying creak. She removed twelve neat bundles of cash and put them into her black vinyl purse as she heard the whine of sirens off in the distance. As she left the store, she also took a pack of Starburst Fruit Chews, some SweetTarts and a pack of Doublemint gum.

One week later, Nadir Abbas returned to his native land, only to find that it was now a wholly-owned subsidiary of the United States of America.

14

Beautiful People

THE LINE IN FRONT of Mixtique stretched for three blocks down Sunset Boulevard. Mixtique was one of those places where the young and attractive pay to mingle with people they might sleep with, but don't necessarily like. Would-be revelers unable to crack the door and gain entrance to Los Angeles' current hot spot were discernable from those on the guest list only by the air of desperation that clung to them like oil on wet pavement, and Nina was determined not to join their ranks.

Over the course of half an hour she had watched the comings and goings in front of the club and had devised a plan audacious, yet economical enough to succeed. Walking boldly to the front of the line she picked the thickest looking dude with a headset that she could find and said:

"I'm supposed to meet Leo DiCaprio and some friends here, but I got detained over at Paramount. Did he come in through this door or through the kitchen tonight?"

Part time bouncer/ full time alcoholic Ray Vincent had a head shaped like a concrete block and eyes as dull as the Orange County weather channel. Like wet granite through an hourglass his mind did the traditional doorman's calculus.

(Editor's Note: Although the following mathematical equation is untranslatable into Standard Written English,

at the editor's insistence a basic symbolic equation is supplied below for the purpose of maintaining fictional clarity.)

GIRL *(Good)* + *CUTE YOUNG GIRL (Real Real Good)*
- LYING ABOUT MEETING FAMOUS PERSON (Bad)
OK

With a snort that communicated nothing, the terminally
intoxicated bouncer let Nina West pass. The interior of
Mixtique had been greatly labored over by two homosexuals
for the better part of six months at a cost roughly double that
of the Gross National Product of Burundi. The lighting,
however, was a shade of pitch black that made discerning
anything in the club next to impossible. If not for the
phosphorescent jewelry worn by a few earthy revelers
imported from the College of Arts and Crafts, there would
have been no light at all.

Nina stumbled over some impeccably shod feet on her
way to the bar where she spent the next twenty minutes trying
to get the attention of one Glen Dennis, a bartender who
exuded indifference like a postal worker on April Fifteenth.
His hair was a great shiny follicle helmet imported from
1983 and anchored in place by a half can of sticky pomade
that ran in the heat and made him look like a sort of effete
Frankenstein Monster. Glen even considered himself a mad
scientist of sorts, although he was never much for conventional
schooling. Instead, he mixed bland potions designed to bring
those starved for alcohol back to the bar looking for a better
booze to mixer ratio. This, they sadly never got.

Nina asked for a Coca-Cola. The bartender shrugged.
She asked again in a louder voice, but he only motioned at
his ears as if to say that hearing her order over the deafening
din was impossible and it clearly wasn't his fault. She leaned

in over the bar, her nascent cleavage fighting for all it was worth to escape from her shirt, and shouted at the top of her lungs:

"Coke! A Coca-Cola!"

Glen Dennis's disdain was palpable. He dissolutely squirted a thin glass half full of flat, warm, brown liquid and placed it in front of her. Flashing all of the fingers on both of his hands and then holding up four fingers on his right hand, he pantomimed the price.

"Fourteen dollars?" Nina asked incredulously.

This time the bartender's ears were miraculously acute, and he nodded in the affirmative. It's been said that a cynic knows the price of everything and the value of nothing. To celebrate the value of nothing, Nina bent down as if to look in her pocketbook and melted back into the crowd that swallowed her up and continued to pulsate, like a mindless amoeba, forever oozing toward a good time.

Her LA nightclub experience had taken Nina from curious to excited and all the way to exasperated in less than an hour. These people were idiots, she decided, Romans at the vomitorium, sipping overpriced drinks while all around them the world went to hell in a handbag. If this was Hollywood, then even Highland Oaks didn't seem as tedious in comparison. Although everyone on this coast thought the Midwest was synonymous with all that was ugly, ignorant, and barbarous, Nina was glad that at least she could add simple figures, read without pictures and occasionally tell the truth if she absolutely had to.

Sighting a square patch of light off in the distance Nina moved toward it, catching tidbits of incoherent party patter as she made her way through the crowd. The atmosphere was loud and oppressive; the layout a nightmare of faulty feng shui; the drone of conversation equal parts mindless and pretentious, which is to say that it mostly centered on the film, television, and music industries.

By the ladies' room another line had formed, almost as long as the one in front of the club. In the time-honored tradition of their mothers and their now depleted mother's mothers before them, giggling cuties queued up to trade gossip and sample each others' excretions huddled close in a porcelain cocoon.

"Oh my God, I just saw DJ Heino spinning, like, Eight-Step Mood Trance in Copenhagen and now he's here with Furry and DoRey on the same night doing Peek-A-Boo House!"

Nina wondered how anyone could tell the difference between one dance track and another. She hadn't heard an actual change in the music all night. It was more like the occasional pregnant pause bathed in cheap sound effects. Eventually, it all gave way to the same repetitive thump that had, at some point when no one was paying attention, replaced melody, harmony and everything else in modern music. It was the type of listening experience that could make her nostalgic even for her late father's Bob Seger and Bruce Springsteen records, and that too was somehow disturbing and sad.

Nina flashed on a scene from an old movie she'd seen featuring a spindly, sensitive guy playing a folk song on the acoustic guitar at a college party. After a few heartfelt lines his guitar is taken from him and smashed against the wall by an irate party guest, who returns the shattered guitar to its owner with a wan, "Sorry," before returning to the dance floor to twist the night away.

15

Controlling the Floor

EVENTUALLY, NINA BECAME AWARE that the line she was standing in hadn't moved an inch since she'd been standing in it and her patience, emaciated on the best of days, had now worn precariously thin. She pulled down her black tights, squatted where she stood and proceeded to urinate on the floor. Between the darkness, the noise and the smoke most of Mixtique's clientele was spared the sight, but her performance did draw some attention from the wide-eyed girls she had been eavesdropping on. When she was through and had wiped herself with a wet square of cocktail napkin Nina looked at them and said:

"Everybody pisses on the dance floor in Ibiza. Just go for it!"

The girls moved closer, and Nina could see that their eyes were as big as saucers, no doubt due to the ingestion of some designer drug, procured over the internet and approved by the Food and Drug Administration only as a dietary supplement. One by one the four helplessly high young ladies converted floor to toilet and in so doing experienced a catharsis unrivaled by anything they had experienced in the last half an hour at least. Best of all, the act of pissing where they stood had created a bond with former stranger Nina. It was a bond that couldn't be broken without the aid of some strong barbiturates and that hobgoblin Time, both of which were in short supply. The moment that Nina realized this was the moment that Nina decided to ruin everything.

"DJ Heino thinks you guys are hot. He invited us to the after party, if you wanna go."

The girls rose as a unit, wiped, giggled and "Oh My Godded" their way in a pack toward the glassed in DJ booth by the back of the club. Nina explained when they got there that the traditional way to signal your approval of the music being played was to remove your shirt and brassiere and jiggle around with all the natural rhythm a drunk Caucasian female can muster. This act might indeed have caused a sensation in the booth if not for the darkness of the club, but the DJs couldn't see two feet in front of them. The drunken group of fraternity pledges from Pasadena standing nearby, however, certainly noticed and began pawing at the half naked girls and trading high fives with each other in the manner of primates discovering for the first time the joy of plantains.

As the girls' giggles turned to screams of mortification Ray Vincent and his cohorts on the security detail descended on the frat boys and began cracking skulls with a randomness that Nina had never before seen. DJ Heino and his cohorts, unaccustomed to such violence in their native Holland, left the booth to try and quell the full-scale brawl that had now erupted on the dance floor. It was a major miscalculation on their part.

There is no activity more pleasing to doormen at a club than beating unmercifully on the clubs' clientele. The wealthy, narcissistic and upwardly mobile are rarely in a position to be so roundly dominated by the drinking, working class as when they have transgressed the unwritten laws of nightclubbing, or even had the misfortune of being within ten feet of anyone who has. And the beat played on.

The beat in all its atavistic primal simplicity, the soundtrack of human mating behavior in our time, played on. Skulls met bottles, fists devoured teeth, boots invaded testicles and the beat played maddeningly, petulantly on. Nina found herself standing in what had become the only safe spot in the club, the now abandoned DJ booth. She looked at the array of electronic gear assembled there; the mixers, turntables, reverbs, effects, and at the records themselves, shiny black in anonymous white sleeves. Maybe there was more to this 'dance music' thing than met the eye, she began to think, before realizing that the eye wasn't the problem. It was what met the ear that was really infuriating. And she wasn't going to stand for it one second more.

Nina grabbed ahold of the turntable's tone arm and cut into the spinning vinyl, producing a sick-making sound that echoed across the cavernous club. For the first time that evening, the place was mercifully beat free. She continued carving the unfortunate record as the bouncers moved the focus of their attention from the students, they were brutalizing to the source of the unnatural sounds coming from the booth. This pause was all the inebriated brothers of Gamma Gnu needed to mount a counterattack that would grow in skill and gallantry with every retelling at the frat house for the rest of the year, eventually eclipsing even their conquest of a dozen inebriated sorority sisters from Lambda Beta Phi.

It was never completely clear who had shot the flare gun that caused the stampede that triggered the sprinkler system that consigned another fabulous nightclub to LA's cultural dustbin. By the time it was over, the Marquise of Queensbury couldn't have sorted out the victors from the losers, and when the police, paramedics and reporters arrived there was still enough senseless violence for everyone. In fact, DJ Heino to this day maintains a civil suit in the county of Los Angeles against Raymond Vincent Jr. who is now a snowboarding instructor in Colorado with no known forwarding address.

Nina decided to take a walk down Sunset Boulevard to try and find something to eat. She was still wandering as the sun came slowly over the horizon and the choke of exhaust fumes and heat swallowed her morning contemplations. A car pulled over and two all-night revelers invited her to take a ride. She thought that she recognized one of them as Dietrich, an orderly from the cast of Doctor's Hospice, but she couldn't be sure as they pulled out of sight.

As much as Nina hated self-reflection of any kind her mind started to wander. After just a few days here, she had to admit that urban California was as much a cultural wasteland as the sanitary suburbs of her mid-Western youth. And although you could always get an avocado sandwich or a pomegranate smoothie here, it was as disappointing as everything else that Hollywood advertised, including its own desperate self.

Her next move came to her as a wood paneled combo van from the nineteen seventies rolled placidly by with two ancient surfboards strapped to the roof and a pair of latter-day Cheech and Chongs passing a joint in the front seat as though the last thirty years had never happened.

16

The Ultimate Solution

OCEAN BEACH THREW SHEETS of baking air off of the sand and up toward a perfect, cloudless sky. Cab fare from the San Diego airport was somewhere in the astronomical range, but for Nina the lure of seeing something quasi-natural, before it was overrun by the young and physically fit was too great to resist. In a pair of shorts and a halter-top, looking as close to sporty as she was capable, she fantasized about weenie roasts around a 1963 campfire. Clean cut young studs frolicked in huarache sandals, while buxom go-go girls in blocky bikinis and industrial strength hairspray danced the Frug and Watusi, their ample breasts jiggling by the campfire's light.

It seemed to Nina that life was easier then, provided you weren't poor, female or a minority of any kind. Come to think of it, life wasn't actually easier then, it just seemed more appealing somehow. The familiar tingle of one of her mind quieting fits came on, and Nina's vision narrowed until the sea was all that she could perceive. She veered off of the asphalt path toward the warm inviting water, kicked off her shoes and plunged in feeling the briny sting of the Pacific Ocean.

Underwater, Nina continued her daydreaming. She was first a shark, then a jellyfish, then an eel with poisonous fangs. She was the Titanic, the Queen Mary, the Pinta, and the Santa Maria, anything but the Nina that she was born to be. As the spell of her musings broke she ran out of air and surfaced, only to feel the sudden blinding thud of something hard and unyielding ramming her skull with enough force to knock her unconscious.

The dreams began again, no longer abstract and infinite, but vivid, immediate. The timeless tide was angry, its rocks impossibly hard and slimy. The sexual salt of the water had become like tempered steel, an immovable wall of oxygen free terror, determined in its huge mindless way to make her its bride, a dead bride in black with white trim.

Lives began to pass before her eyes, lives she hadn't lived and knew nothing about. There was Catherine the Great, a mythical stallion astride her like young Mormons at the Senior Prom. And here was Cleopatra rocking her trademark hairstyle and eye make-up plotting the future of the empire with an asp on one tit and a hapless Macedonian at the other. There was Lizzie Borden and Billie Holiday, Dirty Debby Harry and Mary Queen of Scots and Eleanor Roosevelt, the Patron Saint of Melancholy Lesbians holding court with Annette Funicello and the brassiere that has no end.

And then came Christ. He was well hung beneath his loincloth, uncircumcised and swearing like a sailor. He wore first a milkman's uniform, followed by a cheerleader's skirt and finally an Appalachian's burlap sack. He just stood there half naked, begging quarters for a cup of wine. His eyes were blue, His hair was blond, and He whistled through the holes in his feet.

"Hello, Nina," He said with infinite patience," I hear you've been a very naughty girl."

When Nina awoke she was lying on the sand, the rosebud mouth of surfer nymph Amy Tremain blowing down her throat and into her waterlogged lungs. As consciousness returned, so too did desire. Nina instinctively introduced her tongue into the gaping maw administering life-giving resuscitation. Her chest heaved first with oxygen and then lust as she grabbed a handful of her savior's hair and began to pull at it. Amy's hand reached out toward Nina's parted thighs and the scene began to take shape.

Amy's boyfriend Woody, the owner of the surfboard that had plowed into Nina looked on curiously. In the frantic aftermath of the accident, as he had pulled her limp body to the shore, visions of manslaughter charges had dueled with genuine concern for the victim, but this new development was far better than he could have imagined.

"Rad!" was all he could think to say as he silently wished that Surf World Magazine had an erotic letters page.

Amy Tremain had spent a lifetime trying to prove that she was equal to any dude. When her parents had told her to put on a dress for church she had cried until they'd let her wear Dickey's and a pair of Van's skate shoes. When her brothers told her that she couldn't play baseball she had joined up and then led the league in stolen bases. When she started going to parties on the beach, she hit the beer bong long and hard and left a proud puddle of puke in her wake, then loaded it up and downed it again. But when she had met Woody, it suddenly felt good to be a girl.

Splayed across the warm and unfamiliar sand Nina felt pretty good herself. The taut hardness of Amy's surf enhanced body and the excitement that grew exponentially between the two of them as Nina thrust her finger beneath Amy's one-piece bathing suit promised to turn this good deed into a great one.

Woody knew that this was a once in a lifetime moment, but he couldn't help feeling jealous. This Goth babe, who wasn't even a local, was getting it on with Amy way quicker than he had. And what was he supposed to do now? What if the rest of the crew started calling Amy a rug-muncher and fucking with his head about it? He'd shined a couple of Bettys already on account of her, and he'd be damned if he was going to miss out on this little adventure, but for some reason when he tried to get up and join in, he felt rooted to the spot.

It wasn't that he couldn't do it, that wasn't the thing. He'd never had any trouble getting it up but maintaining it had been a problem ever since Mary Louise Finch took him all the way the summer after 6th grade. Being the gnarliest little dude on the beach had its advantages, but it also made for some pretty weird situations, and her mocking laughter had haunted him every summer since then. Sure, he'd always gotten a lot of action, but he'd also earned the nickname One-Minute-Woody on the unyielding walls of the girls' shower room.

Watching Nina and Amy roll in the sand he felt like his sixty seconds were just about up.

Meanwhile, Amy's ship had sailed. She'd been so turned on at the prospect of saving this girl's life and then making out with her in the sand that she'd climaxed almost immediately and now she lay supine on the beach panting gently under the harsh glare of the sun.

Nina got up slowly and felt the world come back into focus. It was good to be alive, but just barely. She walked slowly to where the surfer boy still sat, his eyes wide, his mouth hanging open like a watery tomb. Nina saw him as he might have appeared 10,000 years ago on this very spot, like a vintage Neanderthal but for the bright red shorts and plastic sunglasses. Nina held her right index finger under his nose and almost smiled. "Shakka," she said.

17

Memories
of a Centerfold

HIGHLAND OAKS WAS SMALL and insignificant outside the window of the wide-bodied jet that touched down and woke Nina West from her airy, recirculated dreams. Within an hour of landing, she was eating ice cream in a bubble bath with the radio drowning out the sound of the television that had been running steadily since her vacation had started five long weeks ago. She hadn't learned much, that was true, but she hadn't forgotten anything either and that had to count for something.

It was then that a ringing doorbell shattered the mood. Glad to be home and even gladder to have the whole house to herself, Nina dragged her dripping form down the hallway ready to hate whoever stood between her and her first evening alone in over a month. With wire bound teeth clenched tightly and blood boiling in righteous indignation she prepared to open fire. But how could she abhor the boy next door?

"Hey Nina, how's it going?"

It had been four long years since Punxby Runninup had left the neighborhood to attend an exclusive military school on the East Coast. For Nina, the dawn of puberty would always be synonymous with the vision of Punxby in his curtain free bedroom pulling bong hits with his buddies from Choton Preparatory Day School. In their ill-fitting suit jackets and thin blue ties they looked like particularly inept FBI agents from 1953, but compared to her then-ten-year-old classmates at Highland Oaks Elementary the boys were both mature and exotic.

Although Nina had no interest in astronomy, she had asked her parents for a telescope and whenever Punxby or one of his friends pulled a dog-eared Playboy from beneath the bed Nina was right there with them, salivating over the buxom blondes and fiery redheads within. This powerful combination of formative influences eventually made of Nina a prodigious masturbator as well as an expert on First Amendment issues and the very newest in car stereos. Once, during a particularly nasty bout of fever, she had even dreamed of cutting Hef's testicles off and feeding them to an enormous shark that swam around in a tank behind the Mansion.

"I heard about your folks and everything. That really sucks."

If Punxby had been born in a different era or another country or an alternate plane of existence he might have offered Nina something more tangible than just his condolences. He might have offered to help Nina with the housework. He might have offered to paint the house or cut the grass or clean those stubborn storm drains. He might have at least looked solemnly into the poor girl's eyes and uttered some encouraging words about God working in mysterious ways. As it was the very act of contemplating anything besides his own comfort was so taxing that he followed it up by pulling out a pack of cigarettes as he eyed what remained of the late Mr. West's liquor cabinet.

It was then that the seismic sexual tremor that was Nina West dripping wet in a bath towel finally pierced the drug addled mind of Punxby Runninup.

When his parents had forced him to come over and pay his respects, he had just assumed that Nina would still be ten years old. The sight of this enticing young woman was more than he had bargained for, and way more than he could handle. Fortunately for him Nina belonged to that certain breed of impulse buyer that sees something useless and just has to have it.

"Punxby, help me with my bath."

Young Master Runninup was not what one could reasonably call a high achiever, but the Military Academy kept him physically fit and his habit of cutting methamphetamine with Viagra allowed him to maneuver reasonably well until the sun broke over Highland Oaks and Nina had almost had enough. He lit his 43rd Marlboro of the evening and took a healthy swig from the bottle of single malt scotch that tilted precariously on a table by the bed. Smoke curled and danced across the ceiling by the dawn's dirty light.

Nina was glad that he both smoked and drank because it meant that he would die that much sooner.

"Punxby, what do you want to be?" she asked, carefully avoiding the suffix 'when you grow up' because she knew that he never would. "Huh?"

"What do you want to be?"

"I wanna be a cool breeze," he said, and for that one magic moment maybe he was.

Then he fell asleep with the lighted cigarette butt still hanging from his mouth. When the Fire Department arrived, it was mostly for show because Nina had already dragged the flaming mattress out onto the front lawn and beaten it to a pile of downy embers, while Punxby snored on the bedroom floor. In a town like Highland Oaks emergency workers always make an appearance when called by an irate neighbor, if only to be able to say later that they had taken every possible precaution to prevent fire from consuming the whole town. What Nina hadn't counted on was the appearance of Highland Oaks Finest, those gallant men in blue who poke around wherever misery rears its ugly head, hoping to create some more.

"Mind if we come in?"

As a matter of fact, she did mind, but since not talking to policemen had always seemed like the best idea, Nina said nothing as Officers Sandusky and Maitland began pawing at her living room like they owned the place.

18

Suffer the Heat

"I'M OFFICER MAITLAND, THIS is Officer Sandusky. We got a report of some suspicious activity so we're taking a look around."

Without further explanation they began looking in cupboards and behind sofas, in ashtrays and under angle poise lamps. They looked under the television and the stereo and they looked in the hall closet and behind the living room drapes. They pried, jimmied, and burrowed as though the fate of the free world rested on finding something suspicious or incriminating with which to persecute young Nina West. It was only the lack of a bona fide search warrant that stopped them from completely trashing the place and then combing the kitchen for unregistered pastry.

Maitland was thin-lipped with short black hair and a crew cut. The permanent sneer that played around his mouth rendered him an object of fear, scorn, or derision (he preferred fear) depending upon the situation. Sandusky was physically average, his very being a definition of nothingness, so he let Maitland do all of the talking, acting, thinking and dreaming, such as it was, for the both of them.

After a thorough inspection, the pair had found nothing that merited a continued search of the house. Being just sufficiently sensitive to notice Nina's go thither stare,

Maitland was about to vacate the premises with a stern warning about wasting the Police and Fire Departments' valuable time when Punxby Runninup emerged from the back bedroom, bleary eyed and reeling on his spindly legs. He clutched the dregs of last night's Scotch bottle in his hand like a glass teat.

That's when Officer Sandusky leapt into action. He threw Punxby to the ground and slammed his head into the floor with all of the force that his unremarkable body could muster. Then he rammed his knee into the back of the terminally pacified prep school punk and began to strangle the life out of him, flashing back to a particularly nasty incident he'd experienced as a marine during the First Gulf War.

Officer Maitland looked on approvingly concerned only that Punxby might not be in enough pain.

Nina watched with mixed emotions. She enjoyed violence, but not law enforcement, and poor Punxby was lovable in a completely worthless way. She edged over to where Maitland stood salivating, removed the 9mm handgun from the holster that hung at his side, and fired three shots into the ceiling. It was like coming home. She loved the feeling of the hand cannon exploding, the deafening blast that rent the air and the shards of plaster that fell to the floor with a random clatter. Nina couldn't claim to know everything, or even most things, but she did know one thing for sure: violence is great as long as you're not on the receiving end of it.

Private First Class Sandusky (Retired) stopped beating Punxby and prepared to surrender to what was left of the Iraqi army. Officer Maitland instinctively put his hands above his head and prayed that death would be swift and painless, although he had a feeling that he might have some explaining to do in the sweet hereafter.

Nina weighed her options. There was murder, which she would undoubtedly be prosecuted for; escape, which she would undoubtedly be caught attempting; suicide, which no self-respecting narcissist could ever truly consider; and surrender which sucked, but was really the only way.

Handcuffed to Punxby in the back of the squad car Nina considered her dilemma again. Out of school with a full bank account and a suburban home all to herself she was sitting pretty an hour ago. Now she was on her way to the police station where they would ask for her age, transfer her to juvenile hall and call…whom? Her entire family was dead. Even her parent's estate lawyer wouldn't do any good in a criminal case like this. She had no friends, which usually suited her fine, but didn't exactly help in these trying circumstances.

"I better call my Dad," said Punxby, with the resigned air of one who had done so a thousand times before. "He'll know what to do."

Nina's cuffed hands negotiated Punxby's jacket pocket and with difficulty dialed the number he told her to. Squirming like a kitten she managed to hold the phone somewhere near his ear and mouth as the cuffs cut into the translucent skin of her fragile wrists.

"Hey Dad, it's me. If you're home pick up, I'm in some kind of trouble…"

The sentence hung there like a convict on the end of his belt until Nina realized that Punxby had nothing more to say. She hung up the phone and tried to be optimistic but having never done so before she really had no idea where to begin. The squad car came to a halt and the two of them were escorted through a maze of hallways to a large room brightly lit by florescent lights. Officer Maitland pointed to a chair in front of his desk and grunted at Nina to sit down. Sandusky did the same for Punxby.

"Name:"

"Nina West."

"Occupation:"

"None."

Officer Maitland regarded her with a cold contemptuous stare. He really didn't like people in general, and he liked criminals even less. But impersonating a nun was about as low as even a perp could go.

"Listen Miss Fancypants, I've had enough of your lip. You want to set your house on fire and run around with some pimply little drunk that's your business. But in my town, when you start firing guns and blaspheming you're gonna get slapped down hard. Understand?"

As always, Nina understood everything all too well.

19

Bellyring of the Beast

DURING THE BOOKING NINA had lied about her age and Officer Maitland was too consumed with hatred to check her veracity. Now, in a musty jail cell complete with reeking toilet and tiny iron cot she ruminated on the wonders of youth. With any luck she'd be free by tomorrow morning and there would be no calls to the child welfare bureau. If things got too heavy, she could always just cry and tell the Powers That Be she was a poor confused orphan who wasn't even old enough to be out past curfew.

"Fuck you, ya cunt. I'll beat yer fuggin' ass!"

From down the metal hallway Nina heard the unmistakable sound of an immovable object meeting an irresistible force. As both object and force made their way down the tier in a hail of grunts, blows and epithets Nina braced herself for her first encounter with the underclass, criminal division. Then, like Venus in handcuffs, Lorelei Humphrey appeared, bathed in the dirty light of the Highland County Women's Detention Center.

A uniformed matron whose back resembled a Greyhound bus backing into a Pizza Hut pushed a key into the lock like she'd done it all before and shoved the uncooperative inmate into the eight-foot-by-eight-foot cell. When the guard had gone Lorelei looked around. Then she looked around again, first at the toilet, then at the walls, then again at the toilet, then at an earwig that scuttled across the floor and finally at Nina who still lay on the small iron cot regarding her flaking blue fingernails.

"What's shakin', bacon?"

Nina wasn't sure how she should respond but being a speed freak Lorelei was entirely capable of carrying on an extended conversation all by herself.

"These fuggin' yo-yos couldn't find a peso in a Mexican whorehouse, am I right? They got my fuggin' car, they got my boyfriend, they got my fuggin' Kid Rock lighter, but they didn't get this shit!"

Lorelei reached into the crotch of her bright orange county jumpsuit and pulled a small plastic bag out. She threw the bag onto the cot and sat down next to Nina who stifled the urge to recoil in disgust. Why anyone would want to stay awake in a place where sleep was the only answer was more than Nina could fathom. The speed was a dull and cakey yellow, the color of old folk's urine. Lorelei knew from experience there were over 150 hours of internal adventure contained in that sac, and like an aardvark hunting termites on a lonely African plain, she stuck a two-inch pinky nail into the bag and found her nose by sheer instinct.

"This is some shit here, you want some? It tastes like dog shit, but it does the trick, right? Gets you where you wanna go. You don't want it, fug it, more for me, am I right?"

Lorelei took another expert snort from the bag and returned it to its genital hiding place with much fussing and fumbling. When Nina finally got a good look at her she saw that Lorelei was cute in a car crash sort of way and couldn't have been older than 19, although her liver probably qualified as middle aged by now. She was also surprisingly well proportioned for someone who ate once a week whether she needed to or not. Nina was always stunned by how strong genes trumped even the direst of circumstances.

"What are you in here for? Shoplifting, drinking, smoking dope, stalking some dude? I don't care, fug it, you don't owe me shit, right? You'll tell me when you tell me, am I right?"

Lorelei sat on the edge of the cot with her feet dangling over the side. She liked this new girl, whoever the fug she was. She was new and kind of weird, but who wasn't, right? Nina watched as Lorelei paced the cell like a meerkat in heat, her taut legs bristling at the three-step limit imposed by the mildewed walls that encircled them. She smiled nervously showing big white teeth and pink gums.

A lifetime of bad decisions and a complete absence of exercise and nutrition hadn't done Lorelei's external form any harm. An EKG might have shown abnormal brainwaves, a psychiatric evaluation might have shown acute psychosis, even a simple check of her criminal record might have shown her to be an irredeemable sociopath, an accident just waiting to happen again and again and again. Still, contrary to all logic and common sense, she looked better than good, even in shapeless prison duds and ironed out hair.

"I used a gun on a policeman."

Nina really enjoyed the sound of that statement exiting her throat, just as she knew that its deliberate vagueness would inspire an orgy of dot-filling in Lorelei's muddled brain.

"That fuggin' rules. I hit a cop with a flashlight once, but he beat the fug outta me and my boyfriend and my daughter. I got more shit if you want it, I still got some on me. They got my car, fug, they got me..."

"Shut the fuck up, it's the middle of the goddamn night!"

A cacophony of floor pounding and toothbrush scraping ensued as a tier of hooting females cursed and threatened the newly minted pair who drew close to each other on the thin prison mattress. Lorelei began to make out with Nina who tore at her cellmate until the floor was littered with bright orange scraps of county jumpsuit. Although they had nothing in common, they had quickly found common ground. Within minutes Nina was plunging headfirst into Lorelei who had presciently cadged a full body wax from a hairdresser she had sold speed to at the mall the day before.

Nina closed her eyes and savored the tangy darkness that washed over her like death, only better. She didn't taste paradise, but she did taste plastic, accidentally swallowing the bag of powder that Lorelei had hidden deep within.

20
Truth, Justice
and Other Dirty Words

"WEST, YOU'RE UP FOR night court, let's go."

Nina left the naked Lorelei snoring on the cot beside her, dead to the world. She swung her feet to the ground and practically ran out the big iron door and down the tier, her heart thumping, and the blood racing in her ears. She had never ingested drugs before, figuring that something as ridiculous as reality didn't really need artificial augmentation of any kind. Now in the grip of the speed she had swallowed she considered the high cost of rubber bands, the weather in Bombay, acid rain vs. acid washed jeans and how unfair it was for the Baseball Hall of Fame to exclude Pete Rose for something as harmless as gambling.

Never had she cared so deeply for her fellow man, yet been so ready to visit McDonald's with an automatic rifle and put a stop to the madness known as existence and didn't anyone have a pair of pliers to pull these goddamn braces off?

"This court will come to order, the Honorable Judge Franklin presiding."

As sad and sorry as the legal system appears in the harsh light of day, it's only more sordid and septic in the wee hours when anyone who might be paying attention is fast asleep. Judge Franklin presided over the poorest excuse for justice that a predominately white, suburban county could muster. Many were the unfortunate drunks and restraining order scofflaws who found themselves behind bars for weeks because of careless filings and sloppy bench warrants emanating from this unassuming place.

Some judges are known as hard heads, some as softies, others as hanging judges, but the Honorable Judge Walter T. Franklin was unique in being known as a sleeping judge. He routinely dozed off during defense arguments and awoke near the end of the proceedings, assigning guilt or innocence randomly, sometimes simultaneously. Those who questioned his judgment were either ignored or found in contempt as the court clerk rattled off another unfortunate name and the loaded dice of justice were rolled again. When this evening's first defendant approached the bench, Nina was taken aside by an earnest looking young man in an inexpensive suit.

"Hello, Miss…West, is that right? I'm your Public Defender, Rick Rangel. I've read the charges against you. Why exactly did you shoot at the arresting officer?"

Nina regarded Rick Rangel for a moment from behind blood shot saucer eyes. He was clean cut, scrupulous, intelligent, boring, a Martian.

"I killed him because he sucked, Rick. Because he never loved his own mother, let alone me. I shot him because he broke into my house and killed my friend, my best and only friend. He's dead now, and I killed him and I'm glad, do you hear me…"

Nina's voice began to rise as Rick Rangel furrowed his brow and tried to calm her down.

"You haven't killed anybody, Miss West. The arresting Officer, Maitland, is seated right over there, and your associate… Mr. Runninup I believe, is seated with the other defendants..."

"You're insane, you're all trying to kill me…"

Rick Rangel asked himself, as he did just about every day at this time why he worked in the Public Defender's Office. He could have gotten a job at a firm with a decent salary dealing with corporate litigators or entertainment people. Who needed the aggravation of representing these drugged out lowlifes? He had already made up his mind to get out of this shithouse as soon as he could. It had been the hardest three weeks of his life.

"Miss West, you need to calm down and get ahold of yourself. They plan to charge you with illegal possession of a firearm, illegally discharging a firearm, arson, resisting arrest, and possibly some other offenses. We need to start formulating a defense and see what kind of bail can be arranged."

One by one defendants were called to the bench and justice of a type was dispensed. Nina became absorbed with the wonders of her right thumb and studied it from every conceivable angle as Rick Rangel continued to pepper her with questions that she ignored. Finally, when everyone else had had their say, it was her turn.

"Nina West," the bailiff called, and she moved toward the bench as if in a dream.

Judge Franklin was a deeply corrupt, repressed, and cynical man. His sex life for the past few decades had been largely nonexistent, due to a supremely unattractive wife and a general petulant hatred of the human race. He had even given up forcing himself on prostitutes in exchange for more lenient sentences, not because of any pangs of conscience, but because middle age had rendered him effectively impotent. He was not kind, nor wise and he certainly wasn't impulsive, but one look at Nina West and he was hooked. Perhaps it was her resemblance to his granddaughter.

Ordinarily, Nina would have responded to the wolf like stare of the judge with a dismissive grunt and gotten on with her day, but this was no ordinary day for Nina. She studied Franklin closely, noting everything, from the deep creases at his eyebrows to the long white renegade hairs that escaped from his wide nostrils and pendulous ears. And she looked through him, through the officiousness and the petty job, beneath the years of tepid smoldering frustration to the gleaming human essence that shined at his core. She truly loved this old man.

"Your Honor, I'd like to take a few minutes to confer with my client."

"You've had a few minutes, counsel. This isn't a psychiatrist's office. How does your client plead?"

Thoughts raced through the mind of Nina West like a herd of jackalope across the Western Plains. She considered suicide, homicide and Ironside, that old TV show with the cop in a wheelchair. She started to laugh out loud, but big wet tears streamed down her face as she looked up at the judge and said:

"Not guilty!"

A combination of basic survival instincts and late-night reruns had coalesced and provided Nina with the right answer for all accusations no matter whom they are leveled at, whatever the time and wherever the place.

21

The Long Arm

"COUNSEL, HAVE YOU EVEN spoken to your client yet? Does she understand the ramifications of what is going on here?"

"Your Honor, I haven't yet had the opportunity to…"

Judge Franklin didn't like the look of Rick Rangel, Esq. He knew the type, doing PD work for a few months to pad out his resume, then moving on to greener pastures chasing ambulances and tithing tobacco companies. It was clear that this smug smartass didn't really care about the welfare of his client or of the court, or even for justice in general. Of course, the Judge also hated Rangel because he was physically attractive and had his whole life ahead of him.

Nina West looked simultaneously at, through, toward, and beyond Judge Franklin, now clearly smitten with the young defendant. Sure, she looked to be high as a kite, but since 1967 hadn't they all? He saw a warm trusting quality in her, an innocence that defied description. She also had those pert little breasts that stood at attention and said, "pleased to meet you!"

"Mr. Rangel, you are dismissed on the grounds that you have inadequately prepared your client's plea. I'm sending a report to the State Bar concerning your conduct and advise you to be more thorough in your preparations the next time you enter my courtroom. Ms. West, you will accompany me to my chambers so that we can arrange suitable representation for you."

"Your Honor, this is highly irregular, I must insist…"

"Court's adjourned! Bailiff, remove Mr. Rangel."

As Nina followed the Judge to his chambers, she had a vision. First, everything turned a brilliant shade of white and as her eyes cleared, she saw Thomas Jefferson, Benjamin Franklin and Abraham Lincoln cavorting naked in an azure stream. Every last citizen of the United States of America from the first settlers at Jamestown to the current lost generation lined the sandy banks leaping and dancing like pink fish through a bear's paw. Betsy Ross sewed a pair of silk stockings as the Olsen Twins looked on and salivated. Malcolm X and Gary Coleman were there too, staring defiantly into a glorious sun emblazoned with the words, "Don't Tread On Me."

Judge Walter Franklin entered his chambers, reflexively saluted the picture of Dwight Eisenhower on the wall and sat behind his gleaming oak desk. Nina took her top off and sat on the floor, wondering aloud if the Judge wanted to try on the handcuffs she had absent mindedly slipped out of while awaiting justice. Franklin hurried to the door, locked it and removed his robe, revealing a pair of legs so pasty and white that they might have been painted by Norman Rockwell during the Great Depression. His brown socks were held up by matching garters and a $15 watch glowed a sickly digital green on his wrist, but the real story for Nina was the pretty violet panties that covered Judge Walter Franklin's wizened old penis and exposed most of his sagging ancient rump.

"You know what I need Mistress. Please, please!"

Franklin fell to his knees and embraced Nina, his wrinkled face flush with her taut lovely stomach. This was what he lived for, to be cuffed and bound, to feel the lash of a stern girl/child with no regard for his position, no respect for his authority, and no concern for his pathetic, nauseating body.

For her part, Nina was still deep in the grip of the methamphetamine, but her patriotic vision had signaled the waning of her mental high and the true beginning of her physical one. Like anyone, anytime, anywhere who gets put in a cage for the night, Nina West wanted to be free. She also wanted some other things.

"Dismiss all of the charges against me and Punxby. I want a concealed handgun permit and full diplomatic immunity for any crimes I might need to commit in the future. Then arrange to have Officers Maitland and Sandusky brought up on charges of entrapment, corruption and incompetence. And if they're acquitted see that they're assigned to the colored section of town for the rest of their natural lives."

Judge Franklin promised to make the appropriate phone calls first thing in the morning. And although he couldn't personally guarantee her diplomatic immunity, he did know someone from the Peruvian consulate that owed him a favor since a regrettable incident last New Year's Eve involving two kilos of cocaine and a contestant from the Miss Universe pageant. At this point in the proceedings, Judge Franklin was ready to give Nina anything she asked for, everything he had.

"I want only to please you Mistress West, to be owned by you, body and soul!"

Of course, it was clear to Nina by now that Judge Franklin had no soul, but aside from James Brown that could accurately be said about anyone. The question now was just how much of what he thought he wanted could Judge Walter T. Franklin take. And how long could he possibly take it for?

22

Judge Not

NINA SLEPT FOR TWENTY-FOUR hours and awoke with what felt like a coating of hair on her tongue. She lay glued to her bed for close to an hour before rolling out onto the floor with a dull thud. Once again, the ceiling hung above like a planetarium robbed of its stars. Her head was throbbing, and her nose ran and she had the vague and not altogether unpleasant feeling that she had killed a man. Or rather she had witnessed a man taking himself where he wanted, where he needed to go.

Nina was young and full of life. Judge Walter T. Franklin was old and full of...well, it wasn't life. Anyway, he had still been breathing when she left the courthouse to pick up some double "A" batteries and a pacifier, but walking toward the incandescent lights of the 7-Eleven she had had another vision.

This time an ancient man with a long white beard and flowing violet robe descended from the sky and fell to his knees before her. He kissed her feet and then slowly turned to dust and Nina knew then that it was time to go. She stole a carton of milk from the back of a truck that stood idling in the convenience store parking lot, took a generous swig, and began the long trek home.

Like a junior college literary journal Nina's mind played through the descriptive options and submitted them for mental review—a thousand points of light stabbed evening's merciful fog. The sidewalk gurgled and churned like a tar pit in the summer heat. Nina's eyes were saucers full of secrets as she pressed on toward the Sandman's dark embrace. It was the best of times, it was the worst of times, call me Ishmael.

Now a full day's sleep had washed her brain clean, though her body still stank in the afterburn of used amphetamine. Overcome with an instant nostalgia, she went to the porch and got yesterday's paper.

Judge Found Dead

Highland Oaks—Judge Walter T. Franklin was found dead in his office early this morning, the victim of an apparent heart attack. The Judge, a respected former prosecutor and 35-year veteran of the bench, was working late following a nighttime session of the Highland County Fourth Circuit Court when he succumbed.

The exact circumstances of Judge Franklin's death are still being investigated at press time, but foul play has not been ruled out. Bite marks, bruises and lacerations were found on the body and several devices described by local police as "suspicious" were discovered at the scene.

Franklin is survived by his wife Amaryllis and two daughters Francine Marsh and Gladiola Franklin. He graduated from the University of Illinois at Normal and attended law school at Tulane before serving in the U.S. Navy during the Korean War. The respected jurist was a member of the VFW and the Highland Oaks Optimists Club. An avid golfer and croquet player he took the slogan 'no pain, no gain' as his personal motto.

Memorial services for Judge Walter T. Franklin will be held at Our Lady of Perpetual Suffering in Oakwood Springs on Friday at 4PM.

Birds sang in the crook of an elm tree. Bicycles flew down a sidewalk cracked with green grass and tree roots that fought eternally with the cement for ownership of the neighborhood. Highland Oaks was a paradise for the attractive and the ambitious, a haven for those who survived and excelled. People like Nina West, and until yesterday, people like Judge Walter T. Franklin.

Nina didn't cry.

23

Jehovah's Shit List

NINA HAD NEVER THOUGHT about death in any serious way until she had lost her parents. At that point she had concluded that death was a good thing unless it happened to you, in which case it was more like a draw. Now her bout with the Judge had shown her just how little separated the living from the dead and her brush with the penal system had shown her just how precarious freedom could be. Still, what good was a lesson if you actually learned it?

The doorbell rang and against her better judgment she answered it.

"Good Morning. I hope you're not busy. I'd like to take a minute to talk about God's plan for you and me."

If God's plan involved talking to complete strangers about religion at 8:00 a.m. on a Saturday morning than God was completely full of shit and Nina wanted nothing to do with Him. On the other hand, the Lord was known to move in mysterious ways and perhaps this visit was part of some grand design. Despite the long dress and dowdy footwear this little black pilgrim wasn't bad looking in a 1972 Pam Grier meets Rosie Grier sort of a way. Nina showed her in, got her a chair and sat down herself. The silence that ensued was pregnant with possibility, but the words that broke it were predictably uninspired.

"God loves each and every one of us. He wants us to be happy and…"

Nina immediately disengaged from the conversation. Not only didn't she believe in God, she didn't believe in anything that couldn't be mounted or swallowed. Ordinarily she might have feigned interest while silently contemplating the floor and twirling her hair around her finger, but today Nina had something on her mind and this so-called person was going to have to make herself useful on this world for a change.

"I'm sorry to interrupt you, but I'm wondering—why do people die? If God loves us and he really cares, why does he take people and destroy them every day?"

In her short life Charmaine Brown had been a victim of childhood sexual abuse, a runaway, a prostitute, a drug dealer, and a thief. She had seen people die right in front of her and she knew that in most times and places life wasn't worth very much at all. But despite what she had been through, she knew as surely as she was standing here in this spoiled white bitch's living room that life did indeed have value and that death wasn't the end of anything, only the beginning.

"Sometimes life can be cruel, but God is always merciful if we just let Him into our hearts…"

"You sound like a fucking Christmas card, you know that? I'm talking about life and death here. I'm talking about existence, about things that really matter, and you just keep reading from your goddamn script. You're completely brainwashed, can't you see that?"

Nina said this with her usual mixture of absolute certainty and callous disregard for other peoples' feelings. She said it because she hated life and she didn't want any part of the Big Lie anymore. She said it not because she wanted to, but because she had to. And as she said it she felt like the prophets of old must have felt as they railed against the wayward and the unbelieving. Meanwhile, Charmaine Brown was having a religious experience of her own.

She had silently asked the Lord for guidance, for some divine insight on how to deal with this poor misguided girl and He had responded instantly with a certitude that can only come from being the Supreme Ruler of the Universe. In a voice both ancient and stentorian He had commanded Charmaine Brown to beat the living daylights out of Nina West right there in her own suburban living room. To thrash the evil from her so that goodness and light could come coursing through and fill her soul with the boundless beauty of the infinite.

Charmaine had been hearing this voice for years, but it was only in the last few months that she had realized that the voice belonged to Jehovah and not to a visitor from another planet. She had even stopped wearing her tinfoil hat when she went to bed at night and had taken to saying her prayers instead. She had joined the Witnesses after brief but unsatisfying stints with the African Methodists, the Pentecostals, the Hare Krishnas, the Raelians and even the Scientologists whom she discovered proselytizing at a train station in Toledo, Ohio.

She began with a right cross to Nina's pert little nose. Blood began to flow immediately, but Nina was more stunned than hurt. She had never been assaulted before without some type of sexual overtone. Her parents hadn't believed in corporal punishment, and she had always studiously avoided those schoolyard altercations that morphed from verbal abuse to the realm of the physical.

Charmaine, with the power of the Word coursing

through her veins, prepared to hit Nina harder this time with an eye toward crushing her windpipe. For her part, Nina had a full-blown revelation. Like a platypus deprived of water her entire life and then reunited with the murky tributaries of the outback the attack had loosed some primordial instinct in her that had lain dormant before. Without thinking she reached for a candelabra that sat atop the piano she had never attempted to play and swung it hard at Charmaine Brown, relishing the melodious sound of chin music.

24

God Takes a Holiday

CHARMAINE BROWN STOOD A full head taller than Nina, she was more muscular, her reach was longer, and walking up and down the steep driveways of Highland Oaks carrying the Watchtower Magazine had put her in the best shape of her life. Charmaine was also a more experienced fighter, having learned the basics in bus stations, crack houses, foster homes and other places that lily white rebel Nina West had never been exposed to.

A Las Vegas odds maker would have bet it all on Charmaine and written off her fragile, teenage opponent as fair game for the vultures. But life isn't fair and Nina knew from the moment she dragged herself off the floor and mopped the blood that trickled out the side of her mouth that she would emerge victorious from this mindless skirmish. She would prevail and live to tell the tale if she felt like it, or never speak of it again if that was how it had to be.

Nina balled up her hand into a fist that could charitably be described as cute. She aimed it at Charmaine's not so pert nose, closed her eyes and lashed out, missing her mark, and hurtling toward the floor. Nina's hands shot out to break her fall and the impact almost broke her wrists instead. Charmaine Brown kicked her solidly in the head with her sensible shoes and Nina saw a flash of blinding light and then tasted the floor again. This wasn't working out quite the way she had hoped.

Nina reached out spastically to gain her footing and by the sheerest coincidence connected with Charmaine's trick knee sending her toppling over backwards onto a well-padded backside. Without missing a beat Charmaine sent out another kick that connected and sent Nina sprawling again. Charmaine, clearly in her element now, got to her feet, dusted off her brown frock and ambled toward the refrigerator for a snack and perhaps a cold beverage. Nina was down for the count.

God chose this moment, after a lifetime of silence, to speak to Nina West.

"Nina, you look great. I assume you'll outgrow the blue nail polish and the permanent frown, but for now you can pull it off. It's lucky for you that I can't stand Jehovah's Witnesses. All that walking around, ringing doorbells and waking people up…why do they think I invented the weekend anyway?"

Nina resisted the urge to tell God to get to the point.

"What you need to do is get mad. That might be a problem for you because it's different than rolling your eyes or making snotty comments. Try to focus on the fact that the religious fanatic that's rifling through your cold cuts is planning to strangle the life out of you and then raid your parent's medicine cabinet. You might want to consider getting up off your ass and doing something about it."

Nina thought God was being kind of an asshole, but He did have a point.

"Your whole generation is so convinced that 'life sucks', that maybe you need a taste of death every once in a while to remind you of the alternative. I've got a hint for you though—sex, television and cool shoes aren't available in the afterlife, so you might want to stock up in the next five minutes or so."

While appeals to conscience or generational solidarity were useless on Nina, her little pixie ears caught fire when the subject of her creature comforts was raised. Although life in the abstract was a pointless waste of time and violence was uncomfortable and made one sweat and bleed, still there were plenty of things in this life worth fighting for. And absolutely nothing worth dying for.

When next Nina's eyes opened Charmaine Brown's prodigious rump was sticking out of the Hotpoint stainless steel refrigerator that sat in a corner of the West's well-appointed kitchen. Nina silently rose to her feet and walked toward her target grabbing a cast iron frying pan from off the hook where it had hung unused since Nina's parents had died. She hadn't had time to miss them yet, and she didn't want to join them now.

Charmaine was someone that Nina would have preferred to avoid, malign or turn her nose up at, but none of those were options now. It was time to kill her or be killed herself. All of the rage and frustration, the accumulated bile of fifteen years on the planet welled up inside her like a hot cancerous ball and when Charmaine rose out of the cool embrace of the icebox she received a hard blow to the face. For Nina, it was just like coming home.

25

What's Brown and Red All Over

Some are born to violence; others have it thrust upon them. Nina was now an official thruster. Her tiny hands clutched the frying pan like a heavy black teat. Elation ran through her body like an electric charge. She felt alive, exhilarated in a way that none of her previous adventures had come close to. Although this wasn't necessarily better than sex, it certainly boasted some eerie similarities.

For instance, anybody can land a lucky stroke now and again. The real masters have staying power. Charmaine reeled on her thick ankles and swiped at her blood-leaking forehead, cursing her appetite and the godless tramp that stood before her. A sound like dead cats in heat welled up from her throat as she prepared to lash out, but before she could move Nina connected again, sending an arc of red cascading toward the hardwood floor. As Charmaine wobbled unsteadily God spoke to her in a voice like wailing Theremins from a Sci-Fi movie:

"Witness Brown, you must destroy the teen age alien. Her coordinates are Prime Vector Four—Alpha Three-Seventy-Two. The fate of the universe lies in your hands. Have some more pastrami. Jehovah loves you."

Although her conversations with Him were fairly utilitarian Charmaine got tremendous solace from talking to the Creator, and even though her head was reeling and she was still kind of hungry, God had spoken. The little albino girl would have to be eliminated.

Charmaine pulled a carving knife from where it hung on the counter behind her and swung it at Nina's neck. Nina ducked and spun, the blow barely catching her translucent left ear and severing the lower part of the lobe right beneath the earring. The pain both stung and infuriated Nina who flew at Charmaine's throat with the business end of a can opener that hung from a Snoopy magnet on the refrigerator door.

Within ten seconds Charmaine had lost so much blood that further violence was futile. That was why there was so much more to come. Nina began to bob and weave, to jab, stick and move like the fighters she didn't remember paying attention to as they grunted across the television set, back when her father ruled the remote. She felt light in her blood-soaked shoes as she hammered and swung, kicked and gouged, huffed and panted.

Charmaine began to resemble a steer left to hang on a hook in a butcher shop. She no longer struggled except to survive, but there was a part of her that welcomed the end of life on this world and longed for a shot at immortality. Nina had ceased in some basic way to be human and had crossed into that realm where pain double dated with pleasure and conscience feared to tread. The floor was awash in blood, hair and innards, but still Nina stabbed on, as though the fate of the free world rested on the complete destruction of Witness Charmaine Brown (Nineteen Hundred Eighty-Five to the Year of Our Lord Two Thousand and Four.)

When she had beaten the corpse into submission, she felt that familiar, merciful vacuum blanket her mind and wash her synapses clean. Epilepsy had its gentle way with her. No dreams disturbed her trance, no television or radio wailed in the background, only light and shadow, stardust and asteroids.

When next she awoke it was hours later, as the sun started its slow drag toward the horizon. A palpable gloom hung over the prone figure of what once was Charmaine Brown. Nina looked at the body, then looked again. Then she vomited long and hard until every Dorito, every Diet Coke, every Starburst fruit chew inside of her coalesced into a work of modern art that no abstruse collegiate essay could save. Not knowing what else to do she dragged the body to the living room so she wouldn't have to sit there alone.

Nina was now a murderer two times over. The pointless deaths of Leland and Dorothy West had been avenged in the only way the Universe reckons equality, through sheer numbers—two of them for two of us. A flood of memories bubbled over into Nina's brain; day camps and picnics and rides on plastic horses, dentists and coaches, ballet and tap, the first day of school, the end of the line and the last days of our lives on Doctor's Hospice.

For the first time in her life, Nina wept.

26

Dead in the Living Room

NINA WEST HAD JUST finished toweling off and dreaming of an unobserved cigarette when the doorbell rang. She had been playing with herself in the bathtub where the cold embrace of porcelain and the hot flow of water from a European showerhead combined to make everything almost all right. It was with a renewed sense of optimism that she crossed the tiled foyer, but when she opened the door there were Officers Maitland and Sandusky, guns at their sides, badges on their blue leather jackets and mackerel stares clouding their empty eyes.

So this was how it ended, caught red handed by the poorest excuse for law enforcement since Barney Fife met the Keystone Kops? Nina looked at the gun in the holster at Maitland's side and contemplated reaching for it again, this time blowing his brain out the back of his head and stealing his patrol car and partner both. Sure, Sandusky was useless, but since she didn't have a license yet the cop would have to drive.

They could cross the Canadian border posing as tourists and she could dump him over Niagara Falls when he got too tiresome. Up North she would live by her wits and good looks, maybe go into forest management, or wait tables, anything where she could be her own boss. Nina would eat right, exercise and only mate with people that really deserved it. She would be glad just to watch the sun come up every morning and set again at night. Eventually her past life in America would become like a distant dream, hazy with the years and she would retire to write her memoirs, still every bit as cute as the day she was hatched.

Meanwhile, the corpse of Charmaine Brown tortured the corner of Nina's eye. From her spot on the living room floor the lifeless Witness challenged Nina to grab for the gun, to start firing and not give up until Highland Oaks was awash in blood. There are moments in life that call for decisive action and flawless execution. Nina West refused to go out like an amateur, undone by the elementary sleuthing of these public dicks. The time was now, the place was here, and the consequences be damned!

"We picked your friend up drunk at the 7-Eleven, waving his Johnson around and throwing up all over the parking lot. We were gonna let him sleep it off in County Jail, but he's stinking up the back of the patrol car and he kept screaming out your name."

Punxby Runninup came hurtling through the doorway courtesy of Sandusky's boot. He landed in a heap at Nina's feet where he lay like a leech on a wet fingertip. Through a long pregnant pause no one spoke. Officer Maitland thought about how much he hated this town with its fancy houses and stuck-up kids. Officer Sandusky thought about how much he hated Saddam Hussein. Nina tried not to think about the irony of a corpse in the living room.

From the floor Punxby started snoring. Officer Maitland opened his mouth to speak, but nothing came out, so Nina closed the front door in his face and shut the porch light off. Then she held her breath and waited. Eventually, she heard disappearing footsteps and slamming car doors and she knew that the law would never, could never take her alive. She would have to do it herself.

Nina stepped outside to the backyard where a high fence separated the West family from their neighbors. The lawn, once meticulously groomed and fertilized, was now long and overrun with dandelions and crabgrass. One of her life-affirming little mind fits came on and stretched out over a full hour of darkness and light.

When it was over Nina got a shovel from a corrugated metal shed that smelled of gasoline and decomposing shrubbery. A long dead rat fed a colony of ants in the corner by the hedge clippers. Nina looked down at the rodent's corpse and she wanted to cry again. She was rapidly running out of first-time experiences and the act of crying felt so wrong that somehow it just had to be right.

Instead she grabbed the shovel, crossed the yard and started digging a hole.

27

Requiem for a Witness

THE NIGHT WAS DARK and moonless, the air chilly and dry. Highland Oaks prepared for another evening by the television, huddled separately in front of the national fireplace. All except for Nina West, engaged in her very first act of manual labor after a lifetime of blissful indolence. As her soft, pliant muscles worked the land, sweat poured down her milky white body and pooled where her lower back hit bottom. When she had finished, a deep hole lay beside a chest high mound of fresh dirt crawling with microscopic life.

Nina strolled back into the house breathing heavily, not bothering to wipe the mud from the soles of her shoes. She climbed the stairs and entered her parents' room. From a small brown chest of drawers, she procured a loaded nine-millimeter handgun that her father had owned, but only fired once. After being mugged on a business trip to Cleveland he had bought the weapon, but quickly lost interest after taking it to a firing range and dislocating his shoulder imitating Clint Eastwood. Nina liked to think that she slept better knowing that the gun was in the house, but she had never had any trouble sleeping so she couldn't be sure.

As she descended the stairs, she passed the line of framed photos that hung in the stairwell, stopping in front of one that she particularly hated. It showed a four-year-old

Nina clutching the mane of a white pony, her eyes wide with the kind of childish terror that could only look cute to someone who wasn't going through it. There were other photos, too. Pictures of her mother dressed in the height of 1980s fashion, of her father graduating from college, of aunts, uncles, grandparents and other people she didn't know, smiling as they acted out scenes from lives she would never understand. Then her eyes alighted once again on the hated pony picture and for the very first time in her life she lost control.

Nina put her fist through the glass frame knocking the picture off the wall and slicing open the pallid knuckles of her right hand. Then she raked the rest of the pictures off the wall sending smiling faces, ancient memories and broken glass clattering down the stairs, the blood from her hand spattering the walls and carpet. All the while she screamed a deafening scream that tore at her throat until she got so dizzy that she fell down the last few steps coming to rest on the hardwood floor three inches from where Punxby lay, still snoring blissfully and dreaming of a bottle with no bottom and young Nina with no top.

She lay there for a good long time listening to the rhythmic sound of Punxby's breathing and the grunts and groans of the old house as it expanded and contracted like the universe, but with more emptiness. She heard an owl out in the yard and a raccoon clanging around the trash cans outside and suddenly even Nature became an obscene parody of itself; another line to cross, another cross unbearable. She got to her feet and walked to the kitchen where the hefty corpse of Charmaine Brown still lay waiting for salvation.

Nina dragged the body out to the hole she had dug in the yard and tossed it in. Looking down at the body she felt obliged to say a few words about the departed. Since she didn't believe in God she addressed her remarks To Whom It May Concern:

"Here lies Charmaine Brown."

At this point Nina was supposed to say something nice about her victim, whom she knew nothing about. She was also supposed to entreat God, whom she still didn't believe in, to have mercy on her mortal soul, a concept she intuitively distrusted. It was more than a spoiled orphan raised on daytime television could stand, and time was running out. Nina settled for a stab at the obvious.

"She's dead."

Nina West wasn't prone to emotions, but in a way she envied Charmaine. To be young, black, and dead was the dream of her entire generation, raised as they were on gangster rap videos and reruns of *Diff'rent Strokes*, but there was something more to it this time. As she gazed at the body in the hole she simply did not want to exist anymore.

An orgy of clichés leapt to mind. Life was vastly overrated. Death was the new black. Why Be? There was no rhyme or reason, no method to the madness. She took her father's gun, cocked it and stuck it in her wanting mouth.

28

Rot in Heaven

IN NINA'S CAPABLE HANDS the most mundane objects became erotic. A loaded gun—hard, cold, and capable of ending your life in a split second was much more than an object. Her mouth began to work the metal shaft of the gleaming black weapon, a final salute to impending doom and her own unlimited libido. Nina wanted to die, but no force on earth could stop her from getting excited by it. She felt a warm sensation between her legs, a quickening of her breath. Best of all, there was no one around to share it with her.

She sank to her knees still working the gun between bee-stung lips, her hips jerking, her hair flying, her nimble fingers reaching for ecstasy in the mouth of the void. And Nina didn't fantasize as she pawed at herself; there was no visual stimuli that could compete with the giant hole she had become. Inside her sex no light penetrated and gravity had ceased to operate by the laws it was accustomed to obeying elsewhere in the universe. When she finally came it was with a great soundless rattle that shook her suburban lawn like the Highland Oaks Giants encountering the Pom-Pon Majorettes in a hail of steroids and Gatorade.

The force of her orgasm sent her reeling into the hole she had dug, her slim form landing flush on Charmaine Brown's rigor mortis beset booty. Panting in the afterglow

Nina's lips touched Charmaine's and for a brief shining moment all was right with the world. It took a while for Nina to return to her senses, but when she did, she scrambled to her feet hyperventilating with the sheer creepiness of it all. If Life really did come down to the basic elements of Death and Sex then she had now experienced all of the attendant combinations that she cared to, save for one. Perched unsteadily on the corpse Nina spotted the gun she had flung by the mouth of the grave. She took it in her hands again and felt the magic leak out of it. This time when she placed it in her mouth, she was ready.

The world, however, was not.

"Nina?"

Punxby Runninup looked like hell, but you couldn't fault his timing. Prematurely thinning hair stuck up off his sweaty bulb of a head, his moth-eaten letter sweater doing double duty as both overcoat and handkerchief, he tried to comprehend the picture in front of him and failed miserably. Blue eyes swimming in pools of red, ears roaring with the sound of sirens he was unprepared to see Nina standing in a freshly dug grave in her own backyard, a gun in her face and the trigger in her hand.

Punxby had never done a good deed in his life, but he loved Nina as only a lazy, good for nothing piece of shit really can. The last thing he wanted, besides a job or a hobby of any kind, was to see her cry. Having rediscovered her he could not imagine living in this world without her. He could not imagine living in this world anyway, but without her it would really suck.

When he was drunk and tweaking and all alone, he saw her where the windshield was supposed to be. She was an oil slick shaped like the Virgin Mary beneath a freeway overpass, she had gotten under his skin, and he couldn't explain it, could no more fight it than draw a sober breath again. Life is cheap, but Nina just…is.

Punxby walked to the edge of the hole and looked down at Nina. Her pale skin shown bright under the moon, her body sleek beneath the great mound of dirt that stood like a forgotten monument behind her suburban home. She was here now, and she always would be. Punxby climbed into the grave and put one hand on Nina's cheek. The other hand grabbed a handful of her hair and pulled it hard, as he kissed her, not gently. Punxby smelled like cigarettes and stomach acid, Nina like vanilla beans and sweat. He grabbed the gun from her hand and heaved her fragile body from the pit with all of the force that his limp biceps could muster.

"Nina, I love you," said Punxby as he cocked the weapon and blew a three-inch hole through the place where his heart used to be.

He collapsed on top of Charmaine Brown whose dull cow eyes still searched the heavens for signs of intelligent life. Nina looked into the hole she had dug for herself. If she had had a cigarette, she might have lit it then, but she had nothing. Finally, she covered the grave with dirt, no tears clouding her bottomless eyes.

When she had finished she went back inside and turned on the television. A late-night talk show was on. Conrad Selby, who played Dr. Nicholas Tanner on Doctor's Hospice, was explaining how he stayed young by working hard, playing fair and keeping a positive mental attitude.

THE END

ACKNOWLEDGE-MENTS

THE AUTHOR WOULD LIKE to thank Philip Cafaro, Melissa Axelrod, Niagara Detroit, Chris X, Rebecca Jung and all of the friends who helped to make this book possible.